"Damn you," the ... you!" The killer beg ... him from hitting any ... there was only one c ... he would have to risk being hit by a bullet to pull it off.

Lee shot once and splintered the man's arm. "Give it up," he repeated, his grip on the Colt beginning to waver. Still the man fired blindly and Lee aimed again. This time the slug struck the man in the center of his chest and sent him reeling.

APACHE RIFLE

Twenty feet ahead, looking out on the trail where Morgan should have been, stood Walking Toad. He had an arrow nocked and ready. Morgan moved Indian-quiet. The redskin was concentrating on the trail and had his back turned. When Morgan was ten feet away he fired a shot into the dirt a foot from the Indian's shoulder.

Walking Toad jumped as if the shot had hit him. He turned slowly, anger clouding his face.

"Slide the arrows to me," Morgan said. "Now go up the bank slowly. I wouldn't want to have to wound you. I need this job."

BUCKSKIN DOUBLE:

SCATTERGUN

APACHE RIFLES

KIT DALTON

LEISURE BOOKS NEW YORK CITY

A LEISURE BOOK®

August 2007

Published by

Dorchester Publishing Co., Inc.
200 Madison Avenue
New York, NY 10016

Scattergun copyright © 1987 by Kit Dalton
Apache Rifles copyright © 1990 by Chet Cunningham/BookCrafters

ISBN 10: 0-8439-3791-2
ISBN 13: 978-0-8439-3791-6

Visit us on the web at www.dorchesterpub.com.

SCATTERGUN

1

Lee was having a drink with Timothy O'Sullivan when the boy from the telegraph office came in with the yellow envelope. O'Sullivan read the message while the boy waited for a reply. Not many Western Union telegraphs were delivered to Mulligan's Five Points Saloon in Boise, and the drinkers at the long bar craned their necks though it was a fair guess that most of them couldn't read.

"Looks like I'm going to Panama," O'Sullivan said. He pushed the sheet of paper across the table. "Read it for yourself."

Lee read it. Somebody who signed himself Clarence King wanted to know if O'Sullivan could join him on an expedition to Panama. RETURN REPLY REQUESTED, the last line read. It had been sent from New Orleans.

The boy had his book and pencil ready. "Leaving today," O'Sullivan said, and the boy wrote it down.

"Get that off right away, sonny." O'Sullivan flipped a dime to the boy and he dashed out.

O'Sullivan was a tall, skinny Irishman in his late fifties, with graying sandy hair and the pallor of poor health. Now that Matthew Brady was dead, O'Sullivan was the most honored photographer in America.

Medals and awards had come his way but they hadn't made him rich. Lesser men made greater money, with their fashionable portrait studios in big cities, but O'Sullivan could never see himself as a bootlicker in a frock coat and shiny top hat.

Born in Ireland and brought to America as a child, he had learned photography under Brady and Alexander Gardner, had gone on to photograph the Civil War and the Far West. No behind-the-lines photographer, he had shared the hardships of the Northern men who found the great war to save the Union. Wet and cold and bad food had given him consumption, though he insisted that a long stay at a lunger's camp in Arizona had cured him. Lee, a good friend, knew better. Most recently he had been operating a photographic studio on Carson Street, in Boise.

O'Sullivan poured a short drink and sipped it. "You want to take a tour down to Panama? You can come along if you like."

Lee smiled at him. That was O'Sullivan, sure enough: restless and reckless, always with his eye on the far horizon. He liked to think of himself as an adventurer who used a camera instead of a gun.

"Whoa, there," Lee said. "What's this Panama business and who is Clarence King?"

"A man who makes maps of remote places. Clarence is an arrogant man but a fine surveyor and engineer. I told you about him."

Lee nodded.

"He's more than an engineer," O'Sullivan continued. "Some of the work he does for the government doesn't always get in the newspapers, if you know what I mean. He's done a lot of things, but this idea of a canal in Panama has been nagging at him for years. It's the kind of secret everybody knows about, but nobody takes seriously. Now it looks like he's got the money and the official go-ahead."

"A canal across Panama?"

"Or Nicaragua. Clarence thinks the chain of big lakes can be linked by canals to make one big canal coast to coast. Panama is his first choice because it's more direct. One of these days there's going to be a war with Spain. Perhaps it won't come for years, but it will come. We have our eye on Hawaii— Senator Beveridge is pushing hard for annexation— and the Spaniards don't like it. They see it as a threat to the Philippines. If war does come we're going to have to move the fleet, and not around Cape Horn."

To Lee, it sounded so remote from his horse ranch in the foothills of the Bitterroot Range in the northern Rockies. Politics didn't interest him— never had. Even so, some of his friend's excitement was getting to him. After a year of hard work rebuilding Spade Bit—long days and short nights— he felt a sudden wild urge to get up and go.

O'Sullivan looked at his big turnip of a watch. "Got to get moving," he said. "Joe can look after the business. I'm leaving on the first train out. One more time: want to go?"

"Doing what?"

"Any number of things you can do. Clarence will be glad to have you along. We're going to need

9

troubleshooters as much as maps and charts. Maybe more. No need to tell you that Panama isn't New Jersey. Make up your mind, man. You told me yourself the ranch is in fine shape, all the Jack Mormon trouble over and done. Listen to me. This settled life will make you old before your time. Rocking chair will get you if you don't watch out. Well, sir, it's not going to get this Hibernian. What do you say?"

"I say, you're crazy, Tim."

But he knew he was ready to go.

It was five in the morning when Lee mounted the buggy and clambered up next to Sam, the only hand who had volunteered to carry his employer into Boise to meet the eight o'clock train. All along the way Lee wondered if he were doing the right thing. Sure the ranch was in good shape. His hired hands were all good men, any one of them fully capable of running the homestead for the three months he would be gone. He glanced over at Sam. Hardly an hour on the road and he was already nodding off at the reins.

He'd have to remember to give Sam a little something extra with his pay when he returned.

As the two rode in silence, Lee looked off to the east and caught a glimpse of the first rosy glow of sunrise. The cool morning air stung his nose and he found himself pulling his coat a little more snugly around him. In just a few short days a coat would be the last thing he would need. New Orleans, where he and O'Sullivan were to meet King and, he supposed, catch a steamer for Central America, would be hot and humid. And once in Panama, Lee figured he would be sweating like a well-worked horse. Hell, he thought, I ain't even on the train yet, and I'm already looking forward to getting home.

As the sun peeked over the horizon and the air began to warm, Sam awoke from his slumber. Lee had taken the reins after the buggy began to veer, and let the man sleep.

Suddenly, Sam snapped awake. "What! Where the hell are we? Where's my bed?" Lee chuckled and tossed the reins into the man's lap. "Don't you remember, Sam? We caught the first stage out for Siam this morning. We're halfway there."

Sam's fuzzy wide eyes cleared when he realized they were on the trail to Boise. "Shit! I'm sure sorry, Mr. Morgan. I'm just wore out. Guess I must'a dozed off a while."

"No problem," Lee assured him. "Any man with gumption enough to stay up half the night helping me pack and then get up at three in the morning for a four-hour trip to Boise's got a right to a little shuteye along the way. There's a creek around the next bend. Let's take a few minutes to freshen up those horses. I've still got time before I have to meet Tim. The train don't leave till eight."

"Mr. Morgan. I sure don't envy you. That's long and dangerous trip you're planning. Panama! Why, half the country ain't never heard of a place like that. From what I hear the whole place is swarming with skeeters as big as a man's fist, and Indians who'd sooner hack a white man's head off as look at him."

"Don't you worry. I can handle myself. You just look after your own business and mind Spade Bit. I left Luke in charge and he ought to do a damn good job of minding the farm until I get back—if he stays sober, that is. You keep an eye on him, you hear? It ain't that I don't trust him, but once he starts in on drinking he's as ornery as a bear and about as irresponsible as a greenhorn with a pair of six-shooters, If there's any trouble, you head straight for Deputy Chook, not that he'll lift a finger to do anything about it."

The two men led the wagon off the trail and down a long slope to the creek. Without unhitching the mares, Sam led the animals to the edge of the crawling water and let them drink their fill from the cool mountain brook. Sam and Lee dismounted in silence and drank their share a few paces upstream. Lee took off his hat, filled it with water, and poured the cold liquid over his head. "Any colder and it'd be ice," he said. "If that don't wake a man up, nothing will."

After remounting the wagon, Sam wheeled the rig around and the two started once again for the city ahead, the biggest in all of Idaho. Sam checked the sun for the time and urged the horses into a trot.

Soon after, Lee spied a wisp of smoke in the distance and knew they were approaching the town. Lee began to feel a pang in the pit of his stomach, more from nervous anticipation than from hunger. His hurried breakfast had been nothing more than a scalding cup of coffee and a mouthful of jerkey. "I sure hope old Tim ain't in too much of a hurry when we get there," Lee said. "I could sure do with a hot breakfast. Might be the last I see for a long time. Tortillas and beans just ain't no substitute for a belly full of hot eggs and fresh bacon."

"Amen!" said Sam.

The first buildings came into view and from all the activity up ahead, Lee guessed that morning in Boise had been in full swing for some time. Idaho wasn't the most populated state in the West by far.

By the time Lee returned from the Yukon, Idaho was just beginning to burgeon. The territory was still frontier, but it seemed as though people had begun to realize that the gold fields were not the only thing the land had to offer. There were still plenty of miners and drifters to be found, and Lee had had more of his share of trouble with them, but the state had grown to over 20,000 permanent citizens, and more were swarming in every day. Boise itself was the seat of government and was the hub that allowed the rest of the state to thrive. The railroad had contributed greatly to Boise's respectability. New shipments of goods passed through the city daily. New settlers headed west for the open country and the gold fields out west, and the disgruntled never failed to fill the eastbound trains.

"Looks like things are hopping this morning, Sam," Lee said, becoming more alert every second. Lee was fond of the solitude of Spade Bit, but he had to admit that the bustle in Boise made him long for the hard living he had not long before given up.

Maybe this trip would help him get his mind off the series of disasters that had befallen him since moving back to his father's old ranch. If he had thought his return would be taken lightly, he had been dead wrong. His ranch had been burned, his wife brutally murdered by a man he'd probably never catch up to, and he found himself starting from scratch at every turn. If he were not a wealthy man as a result of his exploits in the Yukon he would have given up long ago and gone back to roaming the open country until there was no more open country left to roam. Lee knew that no matter how much he wanted to settle down and raise a family, become a respectable citizen in a law-abiding community, there would always be the lure of the wilderness, the beckoning of a country waiting to be discovered—and dozens of men who wanted nothing more than to see him dead. He was torn between living his life the way others thought was right and moral, and the way that was most natural for him—facing each day as it came and each event as he confronted it. He knew as long as he owned land, had responsibility, others would try their damnedest to take it from him, use him for everything they could get. Maybe living hand to mouth wasn't such a bad life after all.

Sam reined in in front of the squat building where O'Sullivan kept a modest studio for himself and his assistant Joe Wister. The wood frame structure was surely nothing to brag about, and Lee couldn't help but wonder why a man with such expensive taste as O'Sullivan didn't move into a place a bit more accommodating. But Lee considered the man who rented it. O'Sullivan was the rough and ready sort. He had no place to call home, no wife to give him comfort and solace, only a gifted eye for a good photograph and a government commission here and there. The place was really a reflection of the man.

"This here's the place," Lee said, hopping down off the rig even before they had stopped. "Mind the horses, Sam, while I make sure Tim hasn't got the itch to leave without me." Lee stepped up the two rickety steps to the front door and into the building. After a few moments he came out again.

"O'Sullivan's assistant says he's gone down to the cafe on the corner for some breakfast. Let's see if we can catch up to him before he gets there. If I know O'Sullivan, there won't be a bite left to eat if he gets there before us. Don't see how that man stays so skinny when he eats more than one of these mares." Sam wheeled the wagon back in the direction from which they came and coaxed the horses into a quick trot. They pulled up in front of the cafe just as O'Sullivan was about to step through the door.

"Hello, there, Tim O'Sullivan," Lee shouted. "Save some of the grub for us."

"Well, if it ain't Lee Morgan," O'Sullivan called back. "I'd just about figured you'd changed your mind about my little proposal. Glad to see you haven't any more sense than I do. Tie up and join me inside. I'll order coffee for three."

Lee and Sam hitched up and went inside to the large table O'Sullivan had claimed. "Have a seat, Lee. Who's your friend, here?" O'Sullivan asked.

"Sam. Sam Lawton," Sam said, extending his hand. O'Sullivan took it in a firm grip and the three men sat. "Mr. Morgan here dragged me out of the sack at three this morning to tote him out here on this crazy trip." Sam smiled, hoping that Lee knew he was being ribbed.

O'Sullivan looked at Lee. "If all your men are this loyal, your ranch is in good hands, Lee. You oughtn't have a thing to worry about."

"That's just the trouble," Lee said, raking his hand through his dark hair. "Ain't many as good as Sam, here. And there's a few I downright don't trust. But there ain't too many honest men down my way looking for hard work on a horse ranch, not when they hear gold's just laying around for the picking. A man's got to take what he can get."

O'Sullivan looked into his coffee, deep in thought. The waitress came over and the three men ordered a hearty breakfast. Sam had ordered just eggs and toast, but after Lee insisted that the meal was on him, Sam reconsidered and ordered flapjacks and bacon as well.

O'Sullivan was still looking into his coffee when Lee broke away from his conversation with Sam. "You got awful quiet of a sudden, Tim. What's eatin' you?"

"Listen, Lee," O'Sullivan said slowly. "We've known each other for a good long time. And you know once I get an itch for something, no amount of scratching's going to make it go away. I'm sorry if I put you on the spot yesterday. King's trip sounded too good to pass up, but I didn't mean for you to get involved. This trip is likely to be dangerous as hell, and I wouldn't want to see you get hurt or killed on account of my foolishness. If you want to back out, I wouldn't blame you a bit."

"Now wait just a minute," Lee said.

"No, you wait," O'Sullivan said insistently. Sam was looking apprehensively at the two of them. "You got a nice life here. Quiet, peaceful, a nice ranch with plenty of land. The way you talk, Spade Bit can't get along without you for a few months. And there's always the chance that you might not come back at all!" Sam's eyes widened when he heard this last statement.

"Mr. Morgan!" Sam exclaimed. "Are you sure you want to go through with this? The man says you might not even come back. There's a lot of folks back home depending on you."

"There ain't one," Lee said, trying to figure out what Sam was getting at. Sam had nothing to lose except his job if Morgan were to be killed. Maybe not even that if the new owner decided to keep him on. Sam had a reputation as a good worker and was respected by everyone in town. He would have no

16

problem finding work.

"What about Suzanne Clemmons?" Sam said cautiously. "A blind man can see that you've been courting her. Some even say you're fixin' to ask her to marry you."

"Who the hell told you that?" Lee said angrily. "Sue can take care of herself. She has plenty of money and her father can provide her with everything she needs. She needs a man like me for a husband like she needs a hole in the head."

Sam sank back into his chair, exasperated. He'd been trying to convince Lee to stay since he first mentioned the trip the night before. Bringing up Suzanne Clemmons was his last ace. He knew he would risk Lee's anger by appealing to his love for the woman. It was his last shot and he had missed. His arguments exhausted, Sam gave in to the fact that Lee was leaving—maybe forever.

"Now listen here, both of you. I'm made my decision to go and I'm sticking to it. Sam, you're worrying like an old maid. And you, Tim, should know by now that I'm perfectly capable of handling myself. So both of you quit your fussing. The ranch is in capable hands. Suzanne can get along without me for a couple of months, and there's no way in hell that anyone's going to get the drop on me."

"Okay, Lee, you win," O'Sullivan said quietly but cheerfully. "I reckon I was just feeling bad 'cause I twisted your arm to get you into this. I know you're as quick-witted as any man. You can handle yourself, as you say, and it'd sure be a comfort knowing you were around if there were any trouble."

"Then it's settled. Let's pay up and get this show on the road. I couldn't drink another cup of coffee if you held a gun to my head. As it is, I'll be pissing all the way to Mississippi . . . and then some."

After paying for the breakfast and complimenting the waitress, the three left and climbed onto the buckboard. The morning was growing more brilliant and warm, and Lee realized that within an hour he would be on his way to more godforsaken unfamiliar territory. Panama was weeks away, but already Morgan was filled with homesickness and dread.

O'Sullivan stared with his mouth agape when he saw Lee's gear. "What the hell's all this stuff, Lee? The settled life's getting to you. Looks like you got everything here but the barn. We're gonna be traveling light and riding hard as soon as we set foot off this train. We ain't going to have time for the comforts of home. Pull out a bedroll and one bag of gear. Anything else you need King will get for you once we get to Orleans."

Lee looked almost embarrassed as he tossed his shaving kit, a couple of changes of clothes and a few other necessary items into one pack, and unlashed his bedroll.

"Looks like the train's in and waiting," Sam said, half wishing that it wasn't. "What a monster. Just the size of one of those things is enough to scare the shit out of me. Glad it's you that's going and not me. I'll stick with tending horses."

Lee and O'Sullivan chuckled as they rode up. The conductors were pacing the loading platform, minding the cargo, and making sure no one without a ticket managed to hide out aboard the train. Not many dared to stow away. Most men knew that if they were discovered they would immediately be thrown off the train, while it was still moving. Who wanted to be stuck out in the middle of the plains with a broken leg, or worse? The railroad conductors were notoriously vicious when it came to ejecting nonpaying passengers.

After Sam had helped Lee and O'Sullivan unload the light gear, Lee spelled out his instructions. "Make sure this gear is put away when you return. And before you go back to Spade Bit, make sure you stop into town and tell Sue Clemmons what I'm up to. She ain't going to like it a bit, but I'm sure she'll understand if you put it to her gently. And for God's sake, don't let on that I'll be into anything dangerous, or nothing you do'll turn off the tears. Now I'm trusting you to keep an eye on things. First sign of anything suspicious, you take off for the law. I'll take care of anyone who gets out of line when I return. Got it?"

"Yes, sir," Sam snapped. "Don't you worry about a thing, Mr. Morgan. Those hands at the ranch know good and well what kind of man you are. They ain't likely to get out of line. Me and Luke'll see to that."

"You keep an eye on Luke, too, you hear? And keep him away from the bottle."

"You bet," Sam answered cheerfully. "And don't you fret none about Miss Clemmons. I'll keep an eye on her."

"You just keep those eyes to yourself, Samuel," Lee joked, "or I'll pluck 'em out and toast them over a campfire."

"We'd better get on board," O'Sullivan called. "Those conductors are looking mighty impatient."

O'Sullivan let the conductor inspect both tickets, and the two climbed aboard with their bags just as the mighty engine began its first groan. A huge cloud of steam covered the platform, and, for a moment, Sam and the rig were lost in the mist. As it gradually cleared, Sam could make out Morgan through one of the windows. Evidently, O'Sullivan had made this trip so many times that he had no qualms about relinquishing the window seat to Morgan. Lee was lighting a cigar, and looking almost the gentleman riding the fine coach, a big grin covering his face like a kid eating candy. The huge train gave a terrific groan and suddenly lurched forward, then began the slow crawl that would lead it out of the station. Just as Sam turned the rig to ride back through town, he heard a voice through the din.

"Hey, Sam."

"Yeah," he hollered back through the cloud covering the train.

"Try to stay awake on the way home," Morgan called.

And then there was only laughter.

Half a day on the rail and mountain country had melted into a vast prairie that seemed as endless as any ocean. Lee spent his time staring out the window watching the scenery change. There were vast stretches that would have been considered desert except for the sparse vegetation and the few jackrabbits ducking from bush to bush to avoid the watchful eyes of the hawks overhead.

"I wonder why there are no buffalo," Lee mused aloud, and tossed a glance toward O'Sullivan.

"So do the Sioux," O'Sullivan answered, tossing his dime novel on the seat beside him. "Care for a few hands of whist?"

"Cards'll do nicely, but poker's my game," Lee said. "Ever heard of it?"

O'Sullivan was pleased that Lee was back into the spirit of the trip, but kept his musings to himself. "Stud. Five or seven card. Your choice."

"Five," Lee said.

"And no betting will be involved," O'Sullivan said. "I've got a box of matches in my pack. If you brought along a few, we'll be set for days."

"No betting, eh?" queried Lee. "Scared of losing your shirt, Mr. Photographer?"

O'Sullivan passed the cards to Lee to shuffle while he rummaged through his pack for the matches. "Hell, no," he countered. "It's just that there ain't nothing to do on a train 'cept read and play cards. And I'm not about to risk hard feelings between me and my best troubleshooter over a lousy card game between friends. 'Sides, by the time I'm through with you, you'll be begging me for a light and you'll never want to see another deck of cards again as long as you live."

"Which might not be too long if things are as bad as I hear they are in Panama."

O'Sullivan just stared at him and dealt the cards. They passed a few hands before Lee spoke of the trip again.

"Listen, Tim. We've been friends a long time. Sometimes I think too long. Level with me. Just how dangerous is this trip? What are we going up against? Yesterday the whole thing sounded like more fun than work. Today I get the feeling we're going to be riding through the Valley of Death."

"The Jungle of Death," O'Sullivan corrected him with a sly smile.

"I'm serious, Tim," Lee snapped, tossing his cards on the table. "If there's likely to be a lot of shooting down there, I want to know right now. You know I'll work as hard as any man. But if this King fellow has anything crooked up his sleeve, you can count me out right now. I ain't sticking my neck out for some glory-seeking asshole.''

"Whoa! Hold it right there, Lee. Looks like I've put a scare in you. This whole operation is on the up and up. Everything's been cleared with Washington, Columbia, and the Panamanian government. There's nothing illicit about it. I'll admit that King is a bit of a, let us say, showman, and, if I know him, he's probably going to be too enthusiastic for his own good; but he's not out to make a fast buck. I'm sure he wants to keep this expedition as peaceful as possible.

"Now, there is something I haven't told you, and I might as well lay it on the line right now. As I told you yesterday, the government has been tossing this canal idea around for some time now. And don't think there hasn't been a lot of opposition. There's plenty folks feel sorrier for the Indians down there than they do for the ones in this country. If that canal goes through, a lot of people down there are going to lose their homes. Run off their land and away from their livelihood. Maybe even be forced by the government to help build the very thing that's going to cause them so much misery. Most likely those people won't see a cent of profit from the damn thing. Still, it's a beautiful country from what I've heard, despite all the horror stories about malaria, savages wilder than any that were ever in this country, and jungles thick enough to swallow a man whole. And I'm going there to make a record of the place on film before it gets destroyed—even if it kills me.

"Then there are the railroad lobbyists." O'Sullivan licked his lips and stared soberly at Morgan. They'd both completely forgotten about the card game they were so involved in only moments before. "I'm sure you are aware how powerful the railroad companies are in this country. They've got half the Congress in their pockets, and when they want their way, they usually get it. Every one there is American owned. If you think they're powerful here, south of the border they practically run the country. There's no regulation. No one to stop them from running things the way they want. And if someone should dispute their hold, that someone simply disappears. They feed 'em to the crocs, I suspect. That's where my worry lies."

"What are you getting at?" Lee asked.

"Though it's no secret the president wants that canal built eventually, the railroads aren't expecting it this soon. But if word gets out King's planning a surveying expedition, we're going to have every railroad employee in Panama on our backs—along with every Indian owned by them. If word of this expedition gets out, if it reaches Panama before our arrival, we're going to have a god-damned war on our hands."

"I see," Lee said slowly.

"I'm sorry for getting you into this, Lee. But I was desperate to have someone as competent as you go along. I don't know any man more handy with a gun. I wouldn't blame you if you jumped off the train at the first depot and headed straight back for Idaho."

"I've gone this far," Lee said. "As long as you're on the level, I'll stick around. Just don't hide anything from me."

"I promise you, I won't. Besides, there may be no

23

trouble at all. As long as everyone keeps quiet about the purpose of this expedition it should be pretty smooth sailing."

"What's your schedule like? How long before we get to New Orleans? We ain't been gone a half day and already my butt's getting sore from sitting. I'll take a saddle any day."

"We should reach the Mississippi in a couple of days," O'Sullivan said. "From there we make transfers to Cairo, Missouri, pick up a couple of horses, and kick our heels to New Orleans. Shouldn't take more than a week if we ride at a good pace. King knows we can't make it any faster, and by then he ought to have a steamer fully outfitted and enough men to make the party look like a small army."

"An army, huh? Just what I need. This clown'll probably hire every outlaw and thief in the South. He got the James gang booked yet?"

"Very funny, Morgan. Now that that's out in the open, shall I whip you at blackjack for a couple of hours?"

The two sat the rest of the day in silence except for the constant deafening roar of the train. At every depot, they got off, ate a hearty home-cooked meal, and stretched their aching legs. By the time they reached Cairo, Lee was as tired as if he'd just spent a month on a grueling trail drive. Little was said of the expedition, for neither man really knew what to expect once they got to Panama. A sense of dread closed in as the solitude of the train ride allowed each man plenty of time to reflect on the possibilities of what lay ahead.

In Cairo, they purchased two sturdy stallions which they intended to sell once they arrived in New Orleans. After a cheap night in the back room of a boarding house, Lee and O'Sullivan set out for New Orleans at first light the next morning, for once skipping the luxury of a big breakfast.

"This is more like it," Lee said as they reached the outskirts of town, fresh air giving them both renewed energy and excitement. The horses stepped high but Lee could tell that his mount had not seen much time on the open road. Still, he had to admire the powerful gait and the animal's polished chestnut coat.

Lee looked west toward home, watching the flat green expanse of land blend into the blue of distance. As he mused about what Sue Clemmons was doing and how she was taking his abrupt and unannounced departure, he turned to look south at the trail that lay before him. Far ahead, there were towering clouds that seemed to both stretched toward the heavens and hold the ground in an inescapable grip. Within an hour it had started to rain.

It was raining when they rode into New Orleans, not a driving downpour, but a steady drizzle that seemed to turn to steam the instant it hit the cobbled streets. They hadn't seen the sun in three days, and Lee wondered how Orleans came by its reputation as a wild, bustling city when everyone was obviously preoccupied with keeping dry.

"Sure ain't Idaho," Lee mused under his breath.

"That it ain't," replied O'Sullivan. "No one ever said this trip was going to be paradise. At least we'll be dry for a day or two—time enough to get a bath and a hot meal, and maybe a sampling of the legendary ladies of this town."

Lee pulled his parka aside and spat out a wad of tobacco. He found the stub of a week-old cigar in his shirt pocket and went through three matches before getting it lit. He drew long and deep, enjoying the rough, dry taste, then blew a ring of smoke into the mist. They were riding through the outskirts of the city, and already Lee was beginning to feel uncomfortable about his appearance. Not only was he drenched to the skin, he was out of his element. The Rockies were his home, back in the hills of Idaho. Rich, fashion-following city folk would be aghast if they knew of the life he had led, and Lee cared to know nothing of city people who had never spent a night camped out of doors. Carriages filled with ladies and gentlemen who looked like whores and bankers sped quickly by, their occupants staring at the two men on horseback as if they were the main attraction in a carnival sideshow. Lee kept his head bent against the rain, not caring to show his face.

"Where are we meeting King?" Lee asked.

"Hotel called François Orleans. I hope he hasn't give up on us. That delay crossing the Arkansas put us two days behind schedule."

"Think he'd leave without us?"

"Doubt it. King's an impatient sort, but we sent word ahead, and he's smart enough not to head into hostile territory without an armed accompaniment.

"There's other men in New Orleans," Lee replied.

"None as good as you, old chum. And he knows it. He'll be there." O'Sullivan caught himself short and went into a long, pitiful coughing fit. When he finally caught his breath, he muttered, "Damn this consumption. Damn this *weather!*"

2

They passed through town slowly. Lee noted with interest the elaborate ironwork that seemed to adorn every building in town. He'd visited many a city in his lifetime, but none seemed as grand as New Orleans—even if the rain was coming down in sheets. Beyond the closed and shuttered windows, Lee could hear the strains of music coming from the newfanged phonographs, which, he heard, had become all the rage in the more civilized parts of the country. Lee had heard one only once before, at Suzanne Clemmons's house, the day before his wife was murdered. He'd even planned to order one for her birthday, thinking that it was a very suitable gift for a proper lady.

The rain had turned the streets into rivers, and Lee was grateful that they were paved, however crudely. As wet and tired as he was, the last thing he wanted was to have to wade ankle-deep in mud. In the distance, Lee could hear a man and a woman speaking in a language he could not understand. The woman sounded vaguely like a whore he had met while traveling through the Canadian Rockies.

"Sure ain't Idaho," he muttered.

The two drenched travelers rounded a corner and Lee saw the woman he supposed had been speaking standing in a doorway, wearing a dress cut much lower than most respectable women would be seen wearing. From across the street Lee tipped the brim of his hat. The woman just stared and nodded in his direction, but the look in her eyes was beckoning him to her. Just then, O'Sullivan dismounted, and for a second Lee though he might be going to take the woman up on her unvoiced offer.

"This here's the livery. We can leave the horses and walk the rest of the way to the hotel. It's just up the street." They walked the horses into the stable and the livery boy began toweling down the two stallions while Lee and O'Sullivan unhitched their packs. When they were finished, the boy unhitched the saddles and led the horses to separate stalls. When he returned, O'Sullivan paid for a night's board and flipped the boy two bits as a tip.

"Take good care of them animals," he said. "They're gettin' sold, saddle and all, first thing in the morning."

The boy looked at them oddly. "Here to stay?" he inquired, curiously. "If you don't mind me saying, you fellows don't exactly look like the city-lovin' type." He bit down on the coin and shoved it into his pocket.

"You've got a keen eye, son," O'Sullivan said. "But your sense of trust ain't so good." He nodded toward the boy's pocket.

"A fellow learns to take precautions with

strangers around here," the boy said.

"Well, this town's only playing host to us for a day or so. Just as soon as we can get a steamer to Central America, we're heading out."

"You must be with Mr. King," the boy said anxiously.

"You know Clarence?" O'Sullivan suddenly became suspicious.

"Didn't until a couple of weeks ago. Craziest man I ever saw. Got the whole town in an uproar. Rode in and rented a steamer from Captain Johnson, then started loading in enough provisions to supply the whole U.S. Cavalry for a year. And all the time waving around enough big bills to choke a horse. What'd he do, rob the mint?"

"Damn. That's Clarence, all right. Never was one to keep a secret."

"He's kept it a secret, all right. Everybody in town's got their own notion about what he's up to. Some say he's going down there to set up some kind of new government. What the hell's he up to?"

"Sorry, son, I can't tell you any more than you already know. We're going on a little expedition. Let's just leave it at that."

Morgan and O'Sullivan pulled the oilskin hoods back over their heads and stepped out into the driving rain. O'Sullivan gestured up the street without saying a word. Lee followed, walking somberly as if part of some bizarre funeral procession. When they finally reached the hotel, Lee stood with his mouth agape at the size of the structure. It seemed more sculpture than building. The massive brick structure was surrounded on three sides by four levels of the most intricate ironwork Lee had ever seen. Each floor had a wraparound balcony and through most of the windows,

Lee could see the incandescent glow of many new electric lamps. In all his travels, Lee had never seen such wealth and splendor in a hotel.

"This here's the place," O'Sullivan said, as he strode up the three steps to the porch. He looked back when he reached the door and saw Lee staring in awe. "Well, are you coming, or ain't you?" he shouted through the storm. Lee broke out of his trance and climbed the steps to the front door.

As they entered, all eyes in the lobby turned to the two dripping men, then followed them as they walked directly to the main desk.

"May I help you two . . . er . . . gentlemen?" the evening porter asked.

"We're part of the King party," O'Sullivan explained. "Is Mr. King in his room?"

"I believe he is," the porter said, "but most of his hired men are staying at the Lafayette on the next block. You might find their accommodations a bit more . . . affordable."

"Mister, we ain't his hired men. Now, if you'll be so kind as to inform Mr. King that Mr. O'Sullivan and Mr. Morgan have arrived, we'll refrain from starting a brawl in your lovely lobby here."

"Y-y-yes, sir. Bellhop, run to Mr. King's suite and tell him there are two gentlemen here to see him. And hurry." The porter stepped back from the front desk and busied himself with some papers, which he shuffled and reshuffled, trying both to ignore the dripping men and the patrons who looked them over with appraising eyes.

"Timothy! Glad you could make it," King was bellowing from the second floor mezzanine, looking for all the world like he owned the place. "Come up! Come up! My room's just down the corridor." Lee and O'Sullivan took off their wet rain gear and mounted the steps to where King stood. He was a big man, about O'Sullivan's age, and what little hair he still had over his ears had turned pure white. If he hadn't been so jovial he might have seemed threatening to the average man. "Dear Lord, you fellows are drenched. You didn't ride in, did you?"

O'Sullivan nodded. "We've been riding since Cairo. Hit a downpour the first day out and it's been coming down ever since."

"Why didn't you take one of the steamboats down the Mississippi?" King asked.

"We'd have had to wait another day in Cario for one to come along. 'Sides, do we look like the type of folk that can afford a steamboat? Those things are for gamblers and millionaires," O'Sullivan joked.

King slapped him on the back and would have buckled over if his gut had allowed him. "So, this must be the hotshot gunfighter you wired me about."

O'Sullivan reddened with embarrassment and Morgan glared at the man who had the nerves to describe him in those terms. When King looked back and forth between the two he noticed a slight bit of tension and quickly held out his hand. Lee broke into a grin. "I'm Lee Morgan," he said, taking the man's offered hand, "fastest gun in the West. Pleased to make your acquaintance." All three broke into a hearty laugh and King led the pair of travelers into his suit.

To Lee, the room seemed almost palatial. There were three huge windows stretching from ceiling to floor, a crystal chandelier, and furniture that would have suited Louis XIV. There was a huge round table off to the side of the room, and around it were three men in stern-looking suits. All three were holding drinks and thick smoke hung over the table like the rainclouds outside. Over the table were strewn charts and maps of every variety: navigational charts, maps of Panama, maps of the entire world. The three men at the table looked very similar in both demeanor and dress. King introduced Lee and Tim and waved them to two empty chairs. King pointed to each of the men at the table. "This is Joe Wilson, Dave Hampton, and Wendell Newport. They've all come down from Washington to help me get this show on the road. Been helping to organize the expedition and outfit the steamer. They've got supplies coming in from all over the country. Mr. Newport here will be going along with us as a government observer. Someone besides me has to report back to the boys in D.C." King's voice bellowed, but the three men at the table sat as staid as before. "As you can see," King said, "these government fellows don't have much of a sense of humor. It's been strictly business ever since they arrived." He looked at O'Sullivan. "I hope you two are going to liven things up around here."

King grabbed a bottle of whiskey and set up a drink for Lee and O'Sullivan. Then he poured another for himself and held it toward the other men. "Gentlemen, to a safe and prosperous voyage." Everyone drank a shot and then King got down to business. "Tim, Lee," he said. "We've finished charting the course and we were just winding down for the evening. Everyone wants to get to bed early so we can get an early start in the morning. We're pulling out day after tomorrow, as you know, and there's still plenty to do yet. Most of the supples have arrived and have been stowed on board the ship. Whatever doesn't come by tomorrow afternoon, we do without. Tomorrow we spend the day readying the ship and unpacking the supplies we'll need while at sea. Every man is supposed to report for duty at first light tomorrow. That includes both of you. I'll show you around the ship and introduce you to the fellows. They're a good lot. Some are a bit mangy, but they'll do just fine. Morgan, since Tim here has such faith in you, I'm leaving it to you to see that there isn't one bottle of alcohol aboard that boat when we leave. This expedition has the blessings of the United States Government and I'm not going to have it screwed up by a lot of drunk, mutiny-minded gunslingers. We're going in to do a job and I'll be damned if it's not going to get done. The captain of the ship has been instructed that he is to let our party ashore, head back here and report our safe landing to the authorities. We'll have another ship waiting in Balboa to get us safely to Nicaragua, after which we'll each go our separate ways. Mr. Newport and I will head straight for Washington to make our report. But remember, the purpose of this mission is secret now, and there will not be a word of this trip spread to anyone, even after it is over. Understood?"

Every man nodded. "No liquor," Lee mumbled under his breath. "Next thing you know, he'll be tossing cigars overboard."

"Mr. Morgan, do you have something to say?" King asked. He eyed Lee closely.

"No. I'm just muttering to myself. Bad habit I picked up."

"In that case, gentlemen, I think it's about time we got some shut-eye. Tim, I managed to wangle a room for you down the hall. It's not much bigger than a closet, but I assumed you wouldn't mind for two nights. I'm afraid Mr. Morgan will have to find accommodations elsewhere. There're several boarding houses down near the waterfront where most of the men are staying. The Lafayette is about a block away, but a couple of the boys have been holed up in Madam Rosa's just down the street. The rooms are nice but cheap, and for a couple of dollars more, Miss Rosa, I hear, offers a few amenities you might not find near the docks, if you know what I mean."

"I know just what you mean, Mr. King. Does sound a bit more pleasurable than staying holed up with a houseful of filthy, sweating men." Lee stood and retrieved his parka from the coatrack beside the door. Then he walked back to the table and picked up the half bottle of whiskey. "Seeing as you gentlemen are retiring straight away, you won't be needing this." He replaced the cork and smiled at King's scowl as he left the room.

As soon as the door had closed behind him, King turned to O'Sullivan with a piercing stare. "Tim, are you sure you made a wise decision bringing this boy along? Last thing I need on this trip is a smartass who won't obey orders. I'm going to hold you directly responsible if he gets out of line."

"Morgan's an independent sort," O'Sullivan replied, "but I've known him since he was fresh, and he's always been honorable. He might be hard to hold, but he knows what's right and what's wrong. And I've assured him that this whole expedition is on the level. He was a wild one when he was younger, but he's settled now. Got a ranch back in Idaho just south of Boise. Got a nice herd of horses, too . . ."

"I don't give a hoot what he's got. I just don't want some hotshot cowboy with a chip on his shoulder going down there with us, shooting every Indian in sight and spoiling the entire expedition.

This is a very delicate matter, and my reputation is on the line."

"He's aware of that, Clarence. Fact is, it was all I could do to talk him into coming along. He thought *you* might be some scoundrel up to no good. Besides, you need him and you know it. He's got a good head on his shoulders and will work like a dog without complaining. And he's probably handier when it comes to shooting than three of the men you've hired. You'll need that in case there's trouble."

"I suppose you're right, Tim. It's just that I've got a lot at stake in this expedition, and so does the government. They want that canal built. And the sooner the better. If anything should go wrong or if there's any trouble with the authorities down there, it might be years before the damn thing gets going."

"All because the government wants to get ships to the Pacific quickly."

Since Newport had been silent for so long, O'Sullivan was surprised to hear him speak up. "That's not the half of it. Washington thinks there might be considerable profit in building a series of canals across the isthmus. Folks would pay a pretty penny in tolls to get to California without making the overland trek. Not only would travel by ship be safer, but it would take half the time. And merchant ships wouldn't have to make the treacherous trip around the South American cape. There's not a captain in his right mind that wouldn't pay a fee to cross safely. The entire West Coast has become prosperous since old man Sutter cried gold back in '49. People have been coming out in droves and the government wants to keep it that way. The stronger the West Coast is, the greater the hold we will have over it should war come. And believe me, war will come."

"So, there is money involved in this. What does Panama get out of it?"

Newport tilted his head slightly sideways and took a deep drag on his cigar. "Sir, this project will employ thousands of men for years. Any man in Panama who wants a job will have one. This project will feed an entire country and thousands will be lifted out of poverty. All we want in return is control over the passage of vessels. It's as simple as that."

O'Sullivan looked at the man, disbelieving. "And what will happen to this fantastically rich country once the canals are complete?"

Newport bowed his head and downed the last of his whiskey. He did not dare to speculate.

The rain had died down to a heavy mist by the time Lee reached the front door of King's hotel. He threw the parka over his shoulders and stepped out into the street. Lee was thankful for the paved streets. New Orleans was known as a rollicking town that never closed down for the night. Yet, this section of the city was remarkably quiet. Maybe King wants it this way, he thought. To stay out of sight and not make waves with the locals. He was sure many of the men King had hired had no inkling of what the expedition was all about, but King was paying handsome wages that not many would be willing to turn down, no matter what the risk. He wondered how many would be going along and how many would stick with the group if shooting started.

Although the rain had been coming down for days, the air was still hot, and the humidity made matters worse. Before he had walked even half a block, his shirt was sticking to his skin with sweat. Up ahead he again saw the woman he had passed earlier as they rode on horseback into town. But the moment he recognized her, she ducked inside the building. She's a sultry thing, Lee thought, as he looked after her. Suddenly Lee realized that the building she had stepped into was Madam Rosa's. The building was unmarked, but the address was the same as that given to him by King. Lee shrugged and crossed the street.

Lee was almost embarrassed as he walked through the front door. His head was down and he was uncomfortable with the idea of staying at a brothel. It had been weeks since he had been with a woman, and he hadn't paid for one since his Yukon days, when he had spent his idle hours enjoying the pleasures his future wife heartily offered. He was also ashamed because of his rough appearance. Surely the men who frequented Rosa's were some of New Orlean's most respectable citizens, the kind of men who were willing to pay any amount for discretion. In Idaho, nobody did except preachers and married men. But neither did he cherish the embarrassment of being turned away because of his trailworn appearance.

As he entered the empty parlor, he jumped at the sound of the door chimes behind him, and he turned to make sure he had not broken something. Lee was taken aback by the elegance of the place. Heavy draperies hung throughout the room, the furnishings were even more posh than those in the hotel he had just left, and the entire parlor was drenched in a soft golden incandescent light. When he turned around again, Rosa was standing by the doorway of the adjoining room.

"Evening, cowboy," she said gaily. "What can I do for you?" Rosa hugged the doorframe in a sultry pose, her green dress slit well up her ample thigh.

Only her khol-smudged eyes moved, looking him over, trying to determine what to make of him, and more importantly, how much money he had in his pocket. Lee noticed that her face matched her name well. And with fewer years and fewer pounds, she might have been a beautiful woman. As it was, Lee had to search through layer upon layer of powder and rouge for any sign of emotion.

"I'd like a room for the evening . . . with a bath, ma'am," he requested, sheepishly.

"I can see well enough you need the bath, sonny. You got money for the room?"

Lee laughed out loud, and received a rude stare in return. "I'm with the King party," Lee said, quiet once again. "Mr. King said I might find a room here."

"Ah, Mr. King. One of my best customers. He's sent so many boys my way in the past week, I've lost count." Rosa pushed away from the doorframe and approached Lee, her hips elegantly swaying. Extending her hand as if to allow Lee to kiss it, she said, "My name is Rosa Velazquez. Mr. King has a running tab here. I've been taking care of a few of his more valued hands," she remarked, winking slyly. "There's plenty of room here. You can come and go as you please. There's no curfew. I serve a hot breakfast every morning, but the rest of your meals you'll have to rustle up yourself. My girls are the cleanest you'll find anywhere, if that suits your taste, and I ain't met a man yet they didn't suit. Take your gear to room 211. There's a bath at the end of the hall and plenty of towels in your room. I'll send Lisa up to make sure you get dried off properly. And if you can't figure out the plumbing, please, honey, give me a hoot."

Lee nodded his thanks and took the stairs to the

second floor landing, two at a time. Rosa clucked her tongue and returned to the room beyond the parlor.

Lee's room was unlocked but dark. He was about to go back downstairs and ask for a lamp when he remembered where he was. He tossed his bag through the open doorway and fumbled with the wall beside the door until he found the light switch. With a flick of his hand, the room was instantly bathed in a crimson glow. The entire room was furnished in red, from the bedspread to the wallpaper. Lee whistled a note and took a step into the room. It was then that he noticed the movement out of the corner of his eye. In an instant he fell into a crouch and had both of his Colts leveled at the object. Then he began to laugh. Across the room he was aiming at himself in the reflection of a tremendous cheval glass. Lee reholstered his pistols and sighed. All this talk of railroad killers and jungle Indians has got me on edge, he thought. And though happy that no one had seen his foolishness, he was relieved that the long trip had not done anything to dampen his keen eye.

Lee pulled the bottle of whiskey from his parka and hung the wet garment on the coatrack. Then he tilted the bottle back for a long, wet swallow. He recorked the bottle and set it on the dresser, then sent his hat sailing onto the bed and picked up the towels and room key lying on the dresser. After turning off the light and locking the door, Morgan walked down the hall to the bath and filled the tub with water. He stripped off his clothes and threw them in a heap in the corner, then eased into the scalding water, letting it fill the tub around him. Then he turned the brass knobs off and lay back to enjoy the soothing, refreshing water.

After a good scrubdown, he pulled the plug and let

the murky water drain. He toweled down and gathered up his clothes, then headed back for the room. Halfway down the hallway he noticed that the light in his room was on.

Instinctively, he reached for his gun, only to discover that nothing was around his waist but a towel. He pulled one of the Colts out of the wad of clothes and made sure it was loaded. He then stood warily beside the door, listening for some indication of who and how many were inside the room. He heard nothing. Morgan gently laid the clothes on the floor beside the door and in one motion kicked open the door and scanned the room with both his eyes and his gun. Just as he was about to squeeze off a round at the figure sitting on the edge of the bed, he realized that it was a woman.

"You must be Mr. Morgan," she said calmly. "Rosa said you might need some help toweling off after that bath. She didn't say anything about getting filled with bullets. I sincerely hope you plan to put that nasty thing away."

"Sorry, Miss," Lee said, laying the gun on the sideboard. "It's just that folks out west don't go sneaking into other folks' rooms without raising some suspicion. No offense, ma'am."

"None taken," she replied, giggling.

"What's so funny?" Lee asked.

"That's a mighty cute little skirt you've got there, Mr. Morgan."

Lee stepped back out into the hallway and retrieved his clothes. When he returned Lisa was sitting in the middle of the bed with her knees tucked under her chin. Lee couldn't help but admire her beauty. She was wearing a tight red cotton dress and her long black hair was tied in the back. She wore no makeup that Lee could see, and that alone made her look a couple of years younger than she really was. Lee figured her about twenty. She's too pretty to be in this business, he thought. But then, he'd thought the same thing about the woman he'd married, too.

Lisa was the kind of woman that men who spent long hours on the range pined for in the evening hours. Most men liked their women full and buxom, with enough flesh to feel like they were holding something. But Lee had a special fondness for small women, especially those as innocent and spritely as Lisa.

After closing the door, Lee moved to the white cane chair in the corner and stared sleepily as she unfastened her bodice. Lee's half-shut eyes widened as he tried to swallow the desert in his mouth as she slid her thin arms out of the sleeves and let the dress drop to her hips. Her small creamy breasts looked back at him, tempting him to come and touch. As Lisa walked toward him, it was desire that pulled him to his feet.

"Lisa," he whispered huskily.

"Hush, now," she answered like a mother to her baby as she pressed her body against him. In a second, Lee's wide hands moved over her waist, caressing the smooth skin of her back and tummy. She nuzzled his thick chest and tickled his salty nipples with the tip of her tongue as she loosened the towel around his waist and let it fall to the floor. "Now is the time for love," she said. "Talk will come later."

She pressed even closer against him and Lee felt his cock begin to fill with lust. He moved one hand from her waist and pushed her dress to the floor.

"Ooooooohhh, Mr. Morgan. I can feel something stirring down there," she said. Then she turned and

43

ran for the bed, Lee hungrily watching her as she dove onto the down mattress and lifted herself to her hands and knees. Playfully, she looked at him from between her smooth legs and in a very girlish voice, said, "Come and get it!" Lee stared at her smiling at him from just beyond the dark wet slit she had been referring to. "Yes, I can see that something is definitely stirring," she teased.

Lee was almost stupified. This innocent young woman was his for the night, compliments of Clarence King, and she seemed to be more than willing to do anything Lee desired—and more. He took a step forward, then hesitated, his organ standing stiff before him, compelling him to take her furiously before she changed her mind.

Lisa turned onto her side and licked one of her fingers. While it was still wet with saliva, she moved it between her legs and pushed it deep into her gaping hole. Her eyes rolled back into her head and she turned over onto her back, furiously masturbating her clit, rolling it between her finger and thumb while Lee stared on.

Quickly, he moved to the bed and lay beside her, replacing her fingers with his own, massaging her clit and feeling the wetness building deep within her.

"Oh, God, Lee, that feels wonderful. Push it in me deeper. Put three fingers in."

Lee silenced her cries momentarily with his lips, exploring her mouth with his tongue. She clasped her arms around his muscular back and pulled him to her tightly. "Lee," she gasped. "I want to taste you. I want that thick thing of yours in my mouth. I want to take it all."

Lisa broke their embrace and gently urged Lee over onto his back. Kneeling beside him, she took his shaft in her hand and slowly began to stroke it.

With her other hand, she caressed his balls and the inside of his thighs. Lee groaned in pleasure at the recapturing of the feeling he had gone so long without. Lisa's tender caresses started out as a tease, but she quickly began stroking him faster, the rod between her fingers straining with each downward stroke. Then her tongue was lapping up the first signs of semen oozing from the swollen, purpling tip. She took the head into her mouth and swung her leg over Lee's head, showing off her cunt right in front of Lee's face. Lee reached up and grabbed her ass. "Come a little closer, honey. I want my tongue inside you. Let me show you how it feels." Lisa complied, almost unconsciously, lowering her pussy onto Lee's mouth.

Lisa was pumping furiously now, her head bobbing up and down, her long black hair spreading over her shoulders. Lee's shaft swelled until he thought it would burst. Just then, Lisa stopped and straddled his cock. "Now I want you in me. I want you to poke that thing of yours into me until I can't stand it any more. I want to feel your love shoot into me."

Lee knew it wouldn't take long. His cock was so hard and red that it was ready to explode at the slightest touch. He couldn't believe what was happening to him. Here was this innocent young thing who looked as if she had just walked off the farm, giving him one of the best and hardest fucks of his life, acting every bit the slut, willing to give him anything he asked for. He couldn't believe his luck. If every woman in New Orleans was this good, Lee thought, he might never go back to Spade Bit.

Lee bucked his hips and plunged his organ deep into her hole. Lisa gave a little gasp and leaned forward, grasping his shoulders and clenching her cunt to give him a tight fit.

"Ooohhh, Lee, push it deeper. That's it. I want every inch of it in me."

Lee pushed her into a sitting position and marveled at her taut little body. He brought his hands to her breasts, alternately caressing them and teasing them with gentle pinches of her swollen nipples. Lisa raked her fingers through the thick mat of hair on his chest, then traced a path down his stomach to the point where their organs ground furiously. She parted her hair to give Lee a better look at the shaft throbbing inside her. It took all the concentration he could muster to keep from coming right then and there. Lisa's eyes rolled back again as she massaged her engorged clit. She was working herself into a frenzy, losing all inhibition and becoming lost in the pleasure of abandon.

"Oh, yes, Lee. You're doing it. Dear Lord, this is the best I've ever had it. Keep pumping me, darling. I'm going to come so sooooon. Ohhhhh. Yes, it's coming."

Lisa had all but forgotten that Lee was even there. All that was left of the world was the excruciating pleasure she was receiving from the cock within her. Her orgasm must have lasted a full minute and then she was hopping up and down on Lee's shaft, trying to bring him to the same climax she had just had. Lee was bucking full force, his shaft almost leaving her opening with each downward stroke. He couldn't remember when he had been so excited, even with his own wife.

All at once he shuddered and felt the hot liquid spurting from the end of his knob. He came for what seemed like forever, wave after wave of ecstasy overcoming him. And when he was spent, he pulled her close to him and held her tightly as much in exhaustion as with relief.

They lay side by side, wordlessly giving each other tender kisses and nibbles, both comforted by the knowledge that the other was fully satisfied. Finally, they drifted off to sleep, Lee dreaming peacefully of a bucolic life in paradise with a wife he would never see again.

It was well before dawn when Lee heard the shots. When he sat bolt upright in the bed, at first he didn't know where he was in the dark. There was a faint light filtering through the window facing the street from one of the dim street lamps. Lee grabbed his trousers off the floor and picked up the gun he had placed on the sideboard. He put the trousers on and quickly fastened the buttons, then tucked the gun into the back of the pants and stepped to the door. He listened for a moment and cracked the door enough to see into the hallway. There was no one there. He moved into the long corridor and stepped gingerly to the landing where he could get a good view of the parlor. Rosa stood in the middle of the room looking up at him with concern and fright evident on her face. She was dressed in a nightgown and robe and Lee could see that she too had been awakened by the shot.

"I heard shooting," he whispered loudly. "What's going on?"

Rosa shrugged, not quite sure that Lee hadn't done the shooting himself. She looked terrified. "Came from up there somewhere," she whispered back.

There was the hurried sound of footsteps coming from the third floor and the unmistakable sound of doors slamming. Lee bounded up to see three heavy-set men standing in the corridor with pistols drawn. "What's going on here?" Lee shouted. The three stared back in consternation, not knowing what was happening.

"Whoa, there, Mister. We heard shots. Sounded like from the room at the end of the hall. We came out to investigate, just like you."

Lee strode past them and stood beside the door. "Friend of yours in there?" Lee asked.

"No. We're bankers . . . from New York. Here on convention. We were going to reserve the whole floor, but that room was already taken when we got here. Got no idea who the fellow is," the eldest of the men said.

Lee tried the door. It was locked. Lee walked to Rosa, who was by now standing, looking every bit terrified, at the top of the stairs. "Give me the key," he demanded. He returned to the room and, without bothering to knock, unlatched the door. He put the key in his pocket and pushed the door open wide. A cool damp breeze hit him immediately, but other than the curtains billowing by the open window, he detected no movement. He put his hand on the wall beside the door and found the light switch. Light flooded the room. Lee noted that it looked very much like his own, and then saw the sleeping figure amid the disheveled bed coverings. He crouched and cautiously approached the bed, while the three bankers and Rosa craned their necks in the doorway to get a better view. There were no closets in the room, no place for someone to hide. When he reached the edge of the bed, Lee rose and aimed his gun at the sleeping form, wondering why the man did not stir. Then he saw the blood. The man's head was covered as if he were having a bad dream, the sheet pulled tightly around him. The pillow was oozing with blood. Lee grabbed the man by the shoulder and turned him onto his back. His eyes stared up lifeless and Lee took a step back as he saw the neat hole in the man's right temple.

He didn't dare look at the other side.

Lee quickly scanned the room. There was the open window leading to the fire escape and Lee noticed the wet footprints leading directly to the bed and back to the window. Lee covered the man's head with the blood-wet sheet. "This man's been murdered. Assassinated is more like it from the looks of things. Rosa, who was this fellow. Was he in some kind of trouble?" Lee asked.

Rosa, who was standing between two of the three men looked as if she were going to faint. The two men took her by the arms and held her up. Then she began to sob violently. "His name was Jim Wilkins," she said. "He was part of the King party, Mr. Morgan. Just like you!"

3

The day dawned glorious and dry. The sun shone brilliantly and seemed to give the city a bright new look. People were in the streets again. Merchants were relieved to have people in their stores again. By 8 A.M. the pier where King's steamer, the Rachel, was docked was crawling with men loading goods and unpacking items that were to be used aboard during the trip. The surveying equipment, the compasses, the spirit levels, the gradienters, current meters and the like were taken to the hold, unpacked, and remained under constant, heavy guard. Food, potable water, medical supplies, and other necessities were kept topside.

King and O'Sullivan were walking about the deck, inspecting the loading procedures and discussing the trip and what led up to King getting the go-ahead. King pulled a gold watch out of his vest pocket and flipped open the lid.

"Eight o'clock. Looks like your man Morgan

51

might have run out on us, Tim. He's well overdue."

"He'll be here. Something must have happened to him. I know it. It's not like him to show up late for a job, especially one of this magnitude. Just give him a little more time. I'm sure he'll have a good explanation."

"He'd better. As I told you before, I'll not tolerate a slouch. I'll lay odds that that good-for-nothing cowboy's wallowing in bed right now with one of Rosa's whores."

"I know better than that. He . . ." O'Sullivan broke off as one of the city's constables stepped across the loading platform and approached the two. O'Sullivan was the first to notice the scowl on the man's face. Thus far the police had stayed out of King's way. As long as there were no laws broken, they were satisfied to allow King to operate any way he wished, even if every city official, from the mayor to the police chief, was craving to know the nature of the operation. All they were told was that it was government business. There were to be no questions asked and no harassment. There had, however, been several arrests, all on charges of public drunkenness. Yet despite the urging of the police, not one of the drunken men revealed anything about what was planned.

"Are you Mr. King?" the constable said, approaching O'Sullivan.

"I am," King butted in before O'Sullivan could open his mouth. "What can I do for you? Is there some trouble?" King suddenly looked very worried.

"I'm afraid there has been," the constable said quietly. "Fellow by the name of Jim Wilkins was killed early this morning, murdered in his bed. There's a fellow named Lee Morgan over at the station who was first on the scene. He and three others at the place heard shooting and discovered the body. The story goes that this Wilkins man was in your employ. I think you had better come with me and answer a few question.''

King looked at the man in consternation. His chubby face reddened and he slammed a clenched fist into his palm. ''Damn!'' he said and shoved his hands into his pockets. ''Very well, I'll go along. This is Timothy O'Sullivan,'' he said, nodding in O'Sullivan's direction. ''He's a good friend of this Morgan fellow. Mind if he comes along?''

''Don't mind a bit,'' the constable answered, ''as long as you think he can be of some help getting this thing solved.''

''I don't know about that,'' King said. ''But I'm sure he can vouch for Mr. Morgan's character. I'm assuming he's not under suspicion.''

''Circumstances don't point to Morgan,'' the constable said. ''In fact, the whole thing's a damn mystery. Everything will be explained to you once we get to the precinct. Now, if you will come along...''

The three men stepped across the gangplank, and King yelled to the foremen to carry on with their duties. O'Sullivan noticed that many of the men who had been working only moments before were now standing idle, watching the scene between the three men. As O'Sullivan turned his back on the scene, he saw the worried look in King's eyes and wondered what had prompted King's change of heart about Morgan. Only minutes before, King was maligning Lee up and down. Now he was taking O'Sullivan along as a ''character witness.''

Despite the beautiful morning, the three men walked tensely and wordlessly toward the station house. As they reached the door, the constable held it open and King and O'Sullivan walked through as if they had just been tried and convicted. Inside, Lee was standing by the front desk. The two men approached him. "Morgan, what the blazes is going on here. What's this about Wilkins being shot last night?" O'Sullivan belted out in a booming voice that raised every eye in the place.

Before Lee could answer, a man in a dark suit stepped into the waiting room. "I thought we'd brought you here to find out just that," the man said, smiling.

"And just who are you?" King asked in a voice almost as loud as O'Sullivan's had been. "And why the hell are you bringing me into this matter?"

"My name is Detective Roy Pinker," the man said. "I've been put in charge of investigating this case and I asked the constable here to bring you in to answer a few questions. I surely didn't think you would object so adamantly, Mr. King. Mr. Wilkins was in your employ, was he not?"

King looked around the room nervously. "Why, yes, he was."

"May I ask who the gentleman accompanying you mgiht be?" Pinker asked.

King puffed up his chest. "This is Timothy O'Sullivan, a good friend of Mr. Morgan's. I thought he might be some help and asked him along."

"Ah, Mr. O'Sullivan. You are quite a celebrity in this part of the country. I've long been an admirer of your work. Your photographs of the West have graced the newspapers here quite often." Pinker sidestepped King and stood directly in front of O'Sullivan. "I understand Mr. King here is planning a little expedition to Central America. A very mysterious expedition, I might add. I assume you are going along to record the adventure on film."

O'Sullivan glanced sideways at King, who was

pleading with O'Sullivan with his eyes, and cleared his throat. He was determined to make the best of a bad situation. "Not exactly, Mr. Pinker. King has his own reasons for journeying where he does. As for myself, I am merely along to photograph whatever may catch my eye, independently of Mr. King, of course."

"I see," said Pinker. "Very well, if you gentlemen will step this way, I'd like to get this over and done with as soon as possible. There's a murderer out there somewhere and I'd like to get this case solved quickly. Mr. Morgan, I was finished with you, but as long as these two gents are here, why don't you step back inside with us?"

Lee shrugged and took off the gunbelt he had just finished refastening, handing it once again to the clerk behind the desk. "I don't like being without my sidearms, Pinker, and I like even less your incriminating line of questioning. I told you before, I've never met this man Wilkins and I don't like it implied that I had anything to do with this murder."

"No one is saying you killed him. I just want to get the facts straight. Murder might be an everyday happening where you come from, Mister, but here in New Orleans we do not take it lightly. Now, if you will leave any weapons you might have with the clerk and follow me, we can get this over with quickly."

The four stepped into a long, narrow side room and were seated around an even narrower table. Pinker took his place at the head of the table. He took out a thin, machine-rolled cigarette and lit up, blowing the first cloud of smoke toward the dim electric light overhead. The smoke hung heavy and the atmosphere quickly becames that of a high-stakes card game, each man looking nervously at the other, wondering what information to volunteer and what to keep secret. To Lee, King seemed almost cowed by this man who spoke so eloquently and reeked intimidation with every gesture. Lee knew it was an act, designed as much to get information about the upcoming expedition as about the case of the murdered man.

Pinker spoke first. "Now, gentlemen, I know little of this secret trip you have planned, and I have been instructed by authorities higher than myself not to ask questions. Mr. King, you have succeeded in setting this entire city on its ears in a matter of two weeks. Rumors are rampant, as I am sure you are aware, and there have been numerous arrests of your men as a result of public drunkenness. To top things off, there are new reports of misconduct coming into this office every day." He stopped and took another drag off the cigarette. Lee noted that it was exactly the kind of dramatic pause Pinker had used on him.

"Now there has been a murder. Not just any murder. Wilkins was shot pointblank through the head—in his sleep, no less. This fact alone leads me to believe that this murder was not an act of passion, but cold-blooded assassination. Now, it is my duty, despite what I have been told, to determine whether or not this act involves your organization. If you have any knowledge of this murder, or if it in any way involves you, I urge you to speak now or suffer greater consequences later. I might warn you that if you are withholding evidence, you and anyone connected with you may be held responsible if and when this case comes to trial."

Now it was O'Sullivan's turn to look worried. He

glanced down at Morgan, who was sitting comfortably with his hands clasped behind his head, a very relaxed posture for a man who might very soon be charged with abetting a murderer. O'Sullivan noted that he seemed to be very sure of himself, as if he held a royal flush against Pinker's pair. Across the table, King simply stared at the detective, an angry, yet frightened look on his face, and waited for Pinker to finish with what he had to say.

"Now, Mr. King. I've dealt the cards. Would you care to ante up?"

King suddenly sat upright in his chair, leaning in closer and trying desperately to muster the courage to respond. "Look here," said King. "I don't know why you are trying to implicate me in this matter. You have been told that this expedition is to remain secret at all costs, and that will stand. I don't care if the whole damn city is murdered. I am not involved, and neither is my crew. In fact, there are only a handful of men who know anything at all about the purpose of this trip. How else do you think it's been kept under wraps for so long? As for Wilkins, yes, he did work for me. He was one of the foremen down at the steamer. Supervised the guarding of supplies. One of my best men, but he was prone to drink. He knew nothing of this expedition, except that we were heading for Central America. I have no reason to believe that his death was in any way connected with this trip. It is far more likely that this was strictly a personal matter, perhaps an unsettled gambling debt, a rejected lover, maybe?"

Pinker broke in. "No woman is going to climb up the side of a building and in through an unlocked window. I neglected to tell you. The culprit gained entry by climbing a rope looped around the building's fire escape. Scaling a wall in blinding rain is not exactly women's work, no matter how determined.''

"I don't give a damn how they got in," King hollered. "I still maintain that whoever did it had no connection with me or my organization. What Wilkins did on his own time, or what trouble he got himself into, was his own business. The same holds true for the other charges you mentioned. These are high-spirited men I've hired, all looking for adventure, and that's just what they'll find with me. But they know that there'll be no drinking or women once we're aboard that ship. Every one of them is out there carousing at night trying his best to get his fill of vice before we shove off. If one of them gets into trouble, you'll have my blessings when you make the arrest. I'll not testify on anyone's behalf. In fact, you'll probably be saving me a lot of trouble in the long run, taking troublemakers off my hands. I've no tolerance for men who cannot obey orders, Mr. Pinker, and most especially when they are under my command.''

"Mr. King, you are beginning to sound very much like a military officer," Pinker put in, and O'Sullivan chuckled at the very thought of King commanding a cavalry regiment or naval vessel. King gave him a burning look that quickly brought O'Sullivan out of his revelry.

"I may be a civilian, Mr. Pinker, but I am under strict orders from the United States Government and I have every intention of carrying out those orders. I wish you the best of luck solving the Wilkins murder and I hope you will give my regards to his family when they have been contacted. Now, if you have no further questions, I am a very busy man and have a ship full of men to look after." King pulled out his watch and after noting the time, slid his chair back as if to rise. Pinker cleared his throat and stubbed out his cigarette as if to indicate that he was not yet through with the men. "Stay seated, please," he said to King, who was looking more agitated every second. "I have no reason to suspect any of you men of wrongdoing, though I am still far from being convinced that the mystery surrounding this expedition has nothing to do with Wilkins's death. Though I have no evidence to hold you, under normal circumstances, I would ask each of you to stay in New Orleans until the case is solved." A worried look crossed King's face and he opened his mouth to object.

"But," said Pinker, "I am inclined to ask just the opposite in this case. King, I want you, your vessel, and your men out of New Orleans by noon tomorrow or, I can assure you, there will be consequences. I'll not have the serenity of this fair city threatened by your continued presence. Do I make myself understood?"

King slid his chair back once again. "I have every intention of doing just that," King said, rising. Now out of danger of being arrested, King seemed deferential to the detective. "I sincerely hope you find your murderer. Your city has been most hospitable. I would hate to leave in the midst of these distressing circumstances." He stretched out his hand to Pinker, and Pinker reluctantly took it. Although Pinker was still suspicious of King, he realized that there was little he could do. The government had tied his hands, and King, he had discovered, was one of the most stubborn men he had ever met.

"I'll accept your innocence for now, Mr. King, but if I get one more hint that you are somehow involved in this, mark my words, government or no government, this expedition is going nowhere."

King nodded and the other two men rose to leave. Lee was the first out the door, walking directly to the clerk to recover his pistols. King lit a fresh cigar while waiting for the two men to collect their arms and glanced back into the room where Pinker stood looking frustrated and helpless.

The three men emerged into the sunlit morning and stood by the edge of the cobbled street until a hansom cab came into view. King flagged it down, waving a bill in his hand, and driver jumped down to open the door. Lee was thinking that with a little time, he could easily adapt to the gentrified ways of the Easterner. Never had he had a man hold a door for him. Back in Idaho, if a man held a door for anyone but a lady, he would have been chased right out of town. Once inside the cab, Lee stretched out his legs, placing his feet beneath the seat facing him. King stuck his head out the window and told the driver to take them to the docks. The driver's eyes widened when he realized who he was transporting. O'Sullivan noted this and wondered if all the citizens of New Orleans considered King with such awe. The man would probably go home that night and tell his wife all about his wealthy passenger, the mystery man the whole town was talking about. Lee was suddenly very serious.

"All right, King, what's this all about? I've been down there since before dawn this morning listening to questions I didn't have the answers to. I'm as willing as the next man to keep this expedition a secret. But I told O'Sullivan on the way here, that I'm only willing to keep my end of the bargain if this thing's on the level." Lee grew red with anger, and looked as if he were going to jump out of his seat and throttle King any second. "You tell me right now who this fellow Wilkins was and what connection he had with you. And don't give me none of that horseshit about him being one of your best foremen. I know a lie when I hear one. And so does Pinker. Only difference is, he's in no position to do anything about it. I am. And if you don't tell me right now what the hell's going on, I'm heading right back there to spill the beans about this whole operation. You understand?"

"Mr. Morgan, there's nothing to tell. As I said . . ."

Lee pulled up his legs and made for the door handle, never taking his eyes off King's worried face.

"All right, all right. Sit down, Mr. Morgan. I admit, you've caught me in a little lie. I can't risk losing you, too. You're too valuable to the success of this expedition."

Lee sat back in his seat and pulled out a cigar, the last of those he had brought with him from Spade Bit. He'd have to pick up another store, perhaps a few Havanas before leaving New Orleans. "That's more like it. Now, just what did you mean by that 'too'?"

King stared at him, wondering how he ever got into this mess. "Just what I said. I can't afford to lose you. I told the truth back there with Pinker." Lee's eyes suddenly narrowed as he suspected that King might be maneuvering his way out of the truth again. "It is true that Wilkins was my best foreman. But that's not the whole story. Wilkins was hired not because of his organizational abilities, although they were considerable, but because he was the handiest man I could find with a gun. Wilkins came out of the cavalry one of the most decorated men since the war. He served mainly on the plains and because of his regiment, settlers have had far fewer troubles with Indians. His tracking abilities were some of the best I've ever seen. I've heard tell of him tracking men, even Indians, over solid rock and through streams. But when he was discharged, there wasn't a job to be found. He hated the West. I guess he'd had enough of it in the Army. His particular skills weren't useful back East. He did get an offer from the Pinkertons, but he turned them down. Not because of the danger involved; in fact, he almost took the job because of that. The fact was that he wanted above all to be his own man. To have no one looking over his shoulder telling him where to go and what to do. He ended up as what I guess you would call a bounty hunter. He brought in many a man and was constantly on the trail of the Jameses and Youngers. Lord knows, I don't know what he'd have done if he ever caught up with them. He always traveled alone and never pined for publicity.

"I met him in St. Louis several years ago and told him about my plans for this expedition. I'd never seen a man more excited about a project so risky. When I finally got the go-ahead, I looked him up immediately, and damn if he wasn't knocking on my hotel door within three days. I signed him up immediately. I had intended for him to go along as my personal bodyguard, but I could use his other skills as well. I let him in on everything and he agreed to pose as a foreman and keep the whole thing quiet. That poor son of a bitch—shot in his own bed. Probably never knew what hit him."

Lee couldn't but notice the lack of sincere concern for the man in King's voice. In all likelihood, Lee thought, King was more concerned with his own safety than that of the dead man. King's interest lay with the expedition and his own vainglory. The loss of Wilkins was just something he would have to accept. Wilkins would have to be replaced, but his death was of no concern.

"Just what did hit him?" Lee asked.

King stuck his head out the window to see that the carriage driver was not eavesdropping. "Surely Tim told you of the potential dangers of this voyage. You've been privy to much information that should not have reached your ears, Mr. Morgan. But as long as O'Sullivan trusts you, I'll deign to do likewise. Although we are merely going to be surveying the Panamanian province, the forces in the railroad industry are willing to do anything to stop us. God only knows how many officials they've bought off down there."

"So I've heard," Lee said, spitting loose tobacco out the carriage window.

"Wilkins was not a man with few enemies," King elaborated. "Fortunately, most of them are either dead or in prison. He knew how to handle himself well, and I believe if he had suspected someone were on his tail, he would not have been so careless as to make their job any easier. Thus, gentlemen, I am inclined to believe that word of the nature of our mission has somehow reached the wrong ears."

O'Sullivan's eyes widened at the thought, yet he remained silent and let the two men finish their discussion.

"How could word have reached Panama and back here in time for them to do anything to stop us?" Lee asked.

"I have no idea, Morgan, and I only pray that I am wrong. If the worst is true, perhaps this is only a warning, intended to scare us off before we even get underway. If so, there may be no further incidents. But no matter what, we shove off at eight tomorrow

—as planned. We'll at least be safe until our arrival, and I'm sure that will tickle Mr. Pinker as well," King chuckled.

O'Sullivan was too aghast to say anything, and Lee was astounded by King's nonchalance and lack of genuine concern. How could he make light of such a situation? There was a man lying dead, and if what King had said were true, there could be many more.

"You seem to be taking this very lightly, King." King stopped laughing.

"No, Morgan, I do not take this lightly. And neither should you. In fact, you should be very concerned for your own safety, as am I. You're the best man I have now and I intend to keep you around. So good, in fact, that I would like you to stay the evening at the hotel tonight. Never mind that there are no rooms. I'll get you one somehow." Lee looked suspiciously at the man, knowing full well that King was merely looking after his own interests.

"Now I see," said O'Sullivan. "I was wondering what brought about your sudden change of heart about Lee once you learned that Wilkins was dead. King, you're more of a conniver than I had ever imagined. Now you want Morgan not only as troubleshooter, but as your own bodyguard. What makes you so sure he wants to look after you?"

King looked askance at O'Sullivan. "The simple fact that I am doubling his salary, effective immediately," said King cheerfully once again.

Lee looked surprised, but not because he needed the money. His income from the ranch and his savings provided him with more than ample earnings. But he was astounded that King would put so much trust in him, a man he hardly knew.

"I accept your offer," Lee said suddenly, but not without generating a harsh look from O'Sullivan. "However, my safety and Tim's safety are my first priorities. I accepted the job as an adventure, not to get my ass blown off. I'll look after your ship . . . and you, but I want a dozen men at my disposal, and they'd damn well better be able to shoot straight. If you're right about the railroads knowing about our arrival, we're in for one hell of a ride."

O'Sullivan couldn't believe what he was hearing. He knew Lee had been brash in his younger years, but he couldn't believe that he would put his life on the line for a man he intensely disliked. He would have to question Lee about his actions later.

The cab pulled up in front of the steamer's gangplank, just as King had instructed. The driver hopped down from the rig to open the door, hoping to receive a large tip for his thoughtfulness. The three men got out of the cab and Lee began to survey the dock and the steamer. Most of the stores of goods had been put away and many of the men were on lunch break, enjoying one of the ship's cook's fine meals, no doubt. Lee stretched after being closed in all morning. In fact, he was pining for the wide open spaces of Idaho. As much as he had admired the city's beauty, he had felt cooped up since his arrival, and he found himself once again longing for home. As he was watching King fishing in his pocket for change to pay the driver, he caught sight of a flash of light from one of the rooftops to his right. When he turned back to the others, he at first saw only the horror registering in King's face. He wondered what the trouble was. Had the man overcharged him? Then the driver slumped to the ground and the shot reached Morgan's ears. Behind where the driver was standing, the man's brains were splattered in an oozing mess over the side of the carriage.

It took several moments for Lee to realize what was happening. King and O'Sullivan were frantically looking for cover and King jumped onto the cab once again just as a slug bit into the dirt where he had been standing.

"Lee, get down," O'Sullivan was shouting from behind a piling. On the steamer, men were running and hollering as if the ship were suddenly under siege. Within seconds, everyone had found cover. By that time, Lee was sprinting toward the building where he had seen the shot. It was a mere fifty yards away and Lee realized that if he hurried, and was lucky enough to not get hit, he might be able to surprise the sniper as he tried to escape down the four flights of stairs. It was a narrow warehouse and there would be no escape from the rooftop, which was not connected to any other structure. The only place the sniper had to go was down, and Lee was determined to see that the man did not reach the back door before he did. Despite O'Sullivan's shouted protests, Lee ran across the open green to the building, like a man possessed. If the man escaped, he would not be caught. Just beyond the building was one of New Orleans' main thoroughfares. If the man reached the street, he could easily slip unnoticed into the crowds.

By the time Lee burst through the entrance of the place, the shooting had stopped. Inside, men were scurrying about as if nothing had happened. The sniper had chosen the location well. The noise from the heavy packing machinery created enough diversion that the men working in the same building had not even realized that there was a gun battle in progress. Lee plowed through, brushing several men aside and ignoring their protests.

"Hey, you. Stop there," a voice bellowed above the other shouts. A huge man stepped in his path, blocking his way to the staircase at the rear of the structure.

"Out of my way, Mister. I'll explain later," Lee said, still coming toward the man.

The man grabbed a long two-by-four and was just about to bean Morgan when Morgan drew. The man dropped the weapon and threw up his hands. Lee rushed past and reached the staircase. The rear entrance was locked and Lee knew that the sniper had no escape except past him. If the man had no weapon except the rifle, Lee would have no trouble getting the drop on him. He knew this was most likely the same man who had killed Wilkins and he was determined not to let him get away.

As Lee reached the fourth floor landing, he paused to catch his breath and wonder why he had not met the killer coming down. Lee kicked open the door leading to the roof and was immediately blinded by a burst of noonday sun. If the killer had been waiting for him, Lee would have been an easy target. Yet, there was no shot. As soon as Lee adjusted his sight from the murky darkness of the stairwell, he eased himself through the opening, brushing off cobwebs and keeping a wary eye scanning the rooftop. He saw nothing. There was no place for a man to hide. Confused, Lee stood on the roof and looked around. There was nothing there but tarpaper and a dozen spent shells at the front of the building where the sniper had been stationed moments before. As Lee waved the all-clear sign to the cowering men below, he saw that the shells were made for long-range, the same kind of regulators used out West. The man had been a professional, obviously hired for the sole purpose of killing. But who his target had been, Morgan had no idea. He could only wonder how the man had escaped him. There was nowhere to go but down.

Lee walked the perimeter of the roof and at the back of the building saw what he had been looking for. There, on the ironwork, was looped a heavy rope, pulled taut. Lee peered cautiously over the edge just as the sniper reached the alley. He wasn't a big man. Lee figured he would have to be agile to scale a rope four flights. His rifle was slung over his back with a heavy canvas strap. Lee took careful aim and yelled for the man to stop. The man did stop, long enough to unsling his rifle. Lee pulled off a round, but the man was a half block away, too far for Lee to hit him. The killer also pulled off a quick round, but it slammed into the side of the building near Morgan's shins. Lee wondered why the man was such a poor shot until he saw that he was standing in the sun. That was his only advantage.

Lee was faced with a tough decision. He could let the man go and hope that Pinker and his men apprehended him. But that was unlikely. Lee's description would not be enough to go on, and in a city as large as New Orleans, there were more than ample places to hide. Or he could go after the man and risk getting his head blown off like the cab driver, as he dangled four floors above the alleyway. But, then, that's what he was getting paid for.

Lee swung his body over the ledge and lowered himself until he had a good grip on the rope. He tried to slide quickly, feeling the skin begin to tear away from his hands. He cursed O'Sullivan silently for making him leave behind the work gloves he had stowed in the gear that went back to the ranch with Sam. Every muscle in his body was strained as he lowered himself to the third floor. The man had taken several more shots at him, all narrowly missing. He must have thought Morgan a fool to chance coming after him, leaving himself wide open and vulnerable. A bullet turned the brick next to his head into powder, the dust getting into his eyes and momentarily blinding him.

It took all of his strength just to hang on. As he passed the third floor, Lee's feet were no longer gripping the rope. He was left hanging in the air wondering what had happened to the rest of the rope. Then he saw the trick. There was no way a man could throw a loop up to the top of a four-story building. He had tied off at the second floor and used a second rope to reach to the roof. With every ounce of strength he could muster, Lee transferred to the second rope and renewed his descent. Still, the man showed no sign of retreating to the street. He was as determined to kill Lee as Lee was to get him. The killer had taken time to reload and was raising the repeating rifle to his shoulder again, as Lee reached the top of the first floor. Every muscle strained as he began to descend hand over hand, anxious to get to the street. The next shot grazed his back and Lee cried out in agony, one hand reflexively reaching to grasp the wound. The sun was no longer in the killer's eyes and he had a clear shot at Morgan. Maddened with rage at having been foiled thus far, the sniper dropped to his knees and took aim. His finger nervously twitched and the shot went high, smashing into the rope that held Lee Morgan ten feet above the earth.

The fraying rope snapped and Lee plunged to the ground. As quickly as a cat, Morgan regained his balance and landed, rolling in the dirt. Flat on his back, he tried desperately to catch his breath. The long train ride and the relaxing day in New Orleans had done nothing to keep him in fighting shape.

"You son of a bitch," the sniper yelled and snapped off three quick rounds. "I'll kill you." Lee rolled again, just as the slugs struck the dirt. He fumbled for his holster and rubbed his eyes to clear the dust.

Lee regained his footing just in time to see the man round the corner of the next block. If the man reached the street at the end of the alley, there would be no chance of catching him, and Lee's efforts would have been in vain.

Lee took off. His legs were in agony from the shock of the fall, but they carried him forward with a determination he did not think possible. He rounded the corner of the alley expecting the man to be long gone, but was greeted instead with a shot that tore a chunk out of his left shoulder.

Lee stood his ground. The sniper's escape route was blocked by debris from the adjacent factory. He was backed up against a pile of brick and rubble that left him no way out except the way he had come in.

Lee leveled his Colt with his good arm at arm's length and took careful aim. "Give it up," he shouted. "Drop the gun." Lee was on the verge of passing out from the pain of the two wounds he had sustained, but he hoped to take the man alive. He was sure he could get the information he needed from him, and even more sure that this was the man who murdered Wilkins.

Lee saw the panic in the man's eyes and knew he would not give up. As a professional killer, he would rather risk certain death than be captured. Like a cornered rat, Lee knew the man would not give up without a fight. And Lee did not have much fight left in him.

"Damn your ass," the man shouted. "Damn you. Damn you. Damn you!" The killer began to fire wildly, rage preventing him from hitting anything more than wind. Lee knew there was only one chance of taking the man alive and he would have to risk being hit by one of the killer's lucky bullets to pull it off.

Lee shot once and splintered the man's arm. He dropped to his knees and Lee could see the tears rolling down the man's cheek.

"Give it up," Lee repeated, his grip on the Colt beginning to waver. Still, the man fired blindly, the barrage of bullets stinging the walls of the alley all around Lee as he moved toward the man.

Lee aimed again at the wounded man. This time the slug struck the man in the center of his chest, breaking his sternum and sending the man reeling onto the pile of bricks behind him. The force of the shot sent him backward and a widening spot of blood shone through his white shirt.

Lee stepped forward to make sure the man was really dead, then he fell flat on his face, unconscious and dreaming of running endlessly toward Suzanne Clemmons's waiting arms, never quite reaching them.

4

"Well, well, Mr. Morgan," Detective Pinker was saying. "I see you've decided to rejoin the living." The man's icy face grinned at Morgan from above.

Lee struggled to focus. His vision was blurred and his head was pounding. He felt as if he had spent the last three days being held prisoner in an opium den. Lee was aware that Pinker was slowly circling him, but he still had no knowledge of where he was or what was happening to him. He shook his head to clear it, but discovered that the movement made it ache all the more.

"Relax, Morgan." Pinker's voice seemed to be booming from every direction at once. "You're in good hands. No one is going to hurt you." With a sudden remembering of the gunfight and the man he had killed, Lee sat up, holding his bandaged head.

"Where am I?" he managed to mutter.

"As I said, you are quite safe," came the reply, somewhat quieter now. "That was quite a little gunfight you had this morning. Very much like home, I imagine.'' The voice seemed mocking now. ''Tell me, do you make it a frequent practice to take the law into your own hands, or do you just have a knack for being where trouble is?''

''Where am I?'' Lee repeated, ignoring the man's remarks. He lifted his hand to the gauze around his head and gasped at the burning sensation that ripped through his arm and shoulder.

''You are in the police infirmary, Mr. Morgan. You should consider yourself very lucky that you are not in the parish morgue.''

Lee was becoming irritated at the man's highbrow tone. ''How did I get here?'' he asked.

''You were carried here, via stretcher. You have received two gunshot wounds, one across your back, and one that tore a good sized chunk out of your shoulder. In addition, you have a rather large lump on your head, which you received when you fell.''

''Fell?'' Lee asked, baffled.

''Surely, Mr. Morgan, you are not suffering from amnesia. The doctor assures me that you are as healthy as a horse. You must remember the events of this morning. You were found, unconscious, in an alleyway next to Steven's Iron Works, a man shot through the chest not five yards from where you lay.''

''Is he . . .''

''Quite dead. I have received a full accounting of the attack upon Mr. King's vessel this morning, and witnesses say you went after the man alone. My interest now is exactly what happened that you should end up half dead in that alley. Just what, may I ask, were you trying to prove?''

Lee glared at the man, not believing that he was

being questioned about having killed a man who would have murdered dozens. "What the hell would you have me do?" Lee asked, the anger rising in his voice now that his senses were returning. "The man was blazing away from the top of that warehouse. He'd killed a man and was aiming for more. Where I come from, folks don't stand by and watch other people get killed without doin' something about it."

"You are in the East, Mr. Morgan. We do have police upon whom citizens can call."

"There was no time," Lee argued. "He would have gotten away. What kind of city is this that would let a murderer run free?"

"Please don't be alarmed, Mr. Morgan. You are not being charged with a crime. I've determined that the man you killed is the same man that murdered Wilkins last night. He had a pistol on his person with the same caliber as that of the bullet removed from Wilkin's skull. And judging from the means of access to the two buildings, I am certain we have our man. I will admit that you have saved me a great deal of detective work, but I would have liked to have taken that man alive."

"I tried," Lee said, his head hanging low. "But he went loco on me. It was either me or him. I winged him, but he just kept firing, and . . ."

"I see," said Pinker. "Tell me, do you still maintain that this man had nothing to do with the King expedition?"

Lee hesitated, wondering whether to continue the charade. "Yes," he stated flatly. "Now, when do I get out of here?"

"You are free to leave at any time. As I said, aside from the wounds I have described, you are quite healthy. Legally, I could retain you for some time, and if it were in my power to do so, I would. However, the mayor and other city officials are very anxious to see you and your party leave posthaste. As I told King, you have until tomorrow noon."

Lee sighed with relief. This city was looking more forbidding every minute. If King didn't leave by morning, Lee decided he would return to Spade Bit without a word. Although still shaky from his ordeal, Lee stood and began to gather his belongings. His head was still groggy and his shoulder and back pounded with pain.

"Mr. Morgan," Pinker was saying. "I would advise you to sit down and wait for the doctor to return with something for the pain." Pinker strode toward the door, then turned to face Lee again. "Just one more thing if I may ask. How is it that you became involved with a man like King? Despite my misgivings about you, I've perceived that you are an honorable man in your own way. You don't seem the sort given to secrecy."

Lee hesitated, then smiled at the man's perceptiveness. "You are right, detective. But I've given my word, and where I come from, a man's word is as good as law."

"Very well, Morgan. I won't pry further. I must say that you lack neither stubbornness nor courage. I trust we will be seeing one another again, perhaps under more favorable circumstances. Good day."

Pinker left the room and, from the open window, Lee watched him walk back to his office until he was out of sight. The doctor came in and checked Lee's bandages, handed him a bottle of tablets for the pain, and told him to stay in bed for the rest of the day and night. Lee shoved the pills into his denim jacket pocket and thanked the man.

Back on the street, Lee immediately pulled the bandages from his head and tossed them into a nearby garbage bin. He raked his fingers through his oily hair and felt the knot just above the hairline. Damn if I'm going to look like a fool with my head taped up, he thought.

He returned to the scene of the killings and noticed that the men were back at work as if nothing out of the ordinary had occurred. There were, however, fewer men aboard the ship and almost everyone stopped to glare at him as he passed, as if to blame him for the incident earlier that morning.

As he stood near the gangplank surveying the scene, an elderly man carrying a bag of flour approached Lee. As he neared, Lee could see that the man had lived a hard life. His face was worn and craggy, with deep ruts and a graying stubble of beard. His hands were twisted from years of labor. He walked with a limp that might have been age rather than injury. His smile as he approached revealed a mouthful of clean white teeth that Lee knew were dentures.

"You're Lee Morgan," the man said, jutting out his gnarled hand. Lee took it and said he was.

"I'm Jim Cook. You'll remember my name because I'm the cook aboard this here heap of rubble." They both chuckled. "Saw what you did this morning. I'm mighty proud to have a man like you aboard. Half of these here men are so green you could plant 'em. Most of 'em have been taking bets all afternoon as to whether or not you was dead. Them that's glaring lost. Personally, I'm glad to see you're still with us."

"I thought they might be blaming me for the incident," Lee said coldly.

Cook's blue eyes sparkled like a young man's. "Hell, no," he said. "You're a damn hero. Ain't nobody blaming you. Some of the boys are getting a mite worried, though. A good dozen walked off right after the shooting—didn't even both to collect their pay."

"Running scared, huh?"

"You bet. Can't say they ain't got good reason, though. Most of them boys got families to care for. Can't blame 'em for wanting to shy from trouble. Mr. King ain't been exactly what you call up front about this trip. A lot of 'em see trouble brewing."

"How 'bout you, pard? You intend to stay on?" Lee asked.

"You betcha. I've been assured this thing's on the up and up, and I'm inclined to believe it. I was a Union foot soldier in the War Between the States, and that's about as low as you can get. But I stood by the flag. If the government wants to go to Timbuktu, I'll be right there with them, no questions asked."

"A true patriot. How about the others? They staying?"

"Like I said, a few of the boys took off at the first hint of trouble. But I think the rest are men enough to stick around. 'Sides, King has promised a healthy bonus to any man who stays on till we reach our destination."

Lee smiled. "Well, we'll see how many stay on when I tell them there will be no liquor hidden away on this ship. If you'll give me a hand, I intend to search this ship right now. And I'd like you to spread the word that any man caught with a bottle will swim home, courtesy of Lee Morgan."

"Hell, you might be out here all night looking for

bottles. Those boys have got 'em stowed away in places I don't even know about. Fact is, I got a couple stashed away myself."

"Then we'd better get started," Lee said, turning toward the boat. "And I'm going to leave it to you to see that no one brings any more aboard this evening. This is going to be one dry boat when we shove off in the morning."

The two men walked on the deck of the steamer and Cook introduced Lee to several of the crew. After exchanging pleasantries, the two men began scouring the ship for whiskey and other contraband. By the time the sun had set, the men had completed one sweep of the ship.

"There's got to be more," said Morgan, but he was too tired to go on.

"Oh, there'll be more, all right. Those fellows are pretty smart when it comes to hiding liquor. I hope you didn't think you were going to get it all. Whad'ya say we call it a night? You need to get some rest. A man in your condition shouldn't even be walking around, much less working. 'Sides; I've got to have supper on the table in an hour. Most of the fellows is eatin' their last meal on shore tonight, but I got to fix up a bit of grub for the ones that want to stay."

"Sounds good to me," Lee said. He smiled at the old man and his feisty attitude. He's probably tougher than any man on board, Lee thought. "I'll be down at first light tomorrow," Lee said as he walked away. "And there'd better not be one drop of alcohol on this ship."

"I'll see to it," Cook yelled. He waved, then turned to walk back to his quarters. Once in the kitchen, he lit an old oil lamp and walked to the stove. Opening it, he plunged his hand into the dark interior, pulled out a bottle of cheap whiskey and uncorked it. "Guess I'll just have to finish it tonight," he mused.

Lee decided against returning directly to the hotel where King and the others were holed up, probably scared out of their wits. The shooting that morning had only served to prove that King was right. Someone was trying to scare them or at least make them delay the trip. There was no doubt that the first shot fired had been intended for King. King was surely aware of that. The murderer was dead, but how many others might there be? Like O'Sullivan had said, the railroads greased the palms of many men. Perhaps even some of the crew could be in their employ. King certainly had not had enough time to check out the background of every man he had taken on. There might be even more deaths before the boat left in the morning. If there were, there was no telling what Pinker might do.

Lee turned these thoughts aside, wanting now only to get safely to Rosa's. When he arrived, he found the door locked. He pounded on it and noted that the burning in his palms had nearly stopped. They were red and blistered, but the slide down the rope had not broken the skin. They were far too calloused for that.

"Who is it?" came the nervous voice from behind the door. Lee recognized it as Rosa's and chuckled at the woman's precautions. "It's Lee Morgan," he yelled. Rosa opened the door a crack to make sure, and then opened it just enough to let Morgan inside.

The room was dimmer than he had remembered and although there was still some light left to the day, all of the curtains were drawn.

"Mr. Morgan, you're all right. I heard there had been a shooting. I was afraid . . ."

"I'm fine, Rosa. Just a few little cuts. Nothing to worry about. I see you've all but boarded yourself in," Lee said.

"Detective Pinker said I might want to take some precautions until you all had left. I'm afraid I don't like shooting very much, especially when it occurs in my establishment. I certainly hope it doesn't hurt business. I'm having enough financial troubles right now as it is. I thought letting you and King's other men stay here might put this business right again. Looks like I couldn't have been more wrong."

Lee saw that the hard edge she had in her voice the night before was nearly gone. Rosa sounded very much like a frightened old woman now.

"Rosa," Lee said, "I've come to collect my things and tell you that I won't be staying tonight. I don't want you to feel that you are in any danger. I just came to pay my respects and say goodbye to both you and Lisa. Is she around?"

"Thank you, Mr. Morgan," Rosa said. "Mr. King's other men said they would spend the night on the boat. Though I have nothing against you, just the same I'm glad you won't be staying. Lisa is out back tending the garden. If you want to go on up and collect your things, I'll fetch her for you and send her to your room."

"Thank you," Lee said, mounting the stairs.

Lee fumbled in his pocket for his key and unlatched the door. Inside, he could still smell the sweet aroma of Lisa's perfume. His bag was still where he had left it and nothing inside had been disturbed. The bed was still unmade and Lee guessed that no one had been in the room since the night before. The curtains were still drawn and the window was shut.

Lee was just putting away the last of his gear, when the door burst open. Lee jumped behind the bed and drew his Colt. He waited to hear a shot. When none came he peeked over the edge and saw Lisa standing in the doorframe, posed with her hand on her hips and smiling at him. She giggled at the sight of him hiding behind the bed, then ran and jumped on the mussed sheets. "Lee, I'm so glad you're safe and back here with me. Let's play." She bounced on the bed, ignoring his worried look.

Lee stood and sat on the bed beside her. She lay back and her mood suddenly changed. "What's wrong, Lee? Don't you like me any more?"

"Of course I like you," he said. "Last night was one of the finest nights I ever spent with any woman. Too bad it had to be interrupted."

"We could continue it now," Lisa said encouragingly.

"No," Lee said. "I would like to, believe me. But I've come to say goodbye and pick up my things. King and I think it might be better if I stay at the hotel tonight. He has a whole floor rented there and everyone will be safer if we stay together. I don't know who else might be trying to get at me or anyone else in King's party. Besides, Rosa is worried sick that someone else is going to break in here and shoot up the place. It's better all around that I leave."

Lee could see the tears forming in Lisa's eyes. He brushed them aside, then looked at her in sympathy.

He was feeling some emotion about leaving this girl as well, but after the morning he would be gone anyway, and there was no way he could take her with him.

Lee suddenly pulled himself together. "Now don't you start crying on me. You ask me to stay one more night and the next thing you know, you'll have me raising a family. I don't belong here. This is your town. My place is the open road."

Lee couldn't believe what he was saying. Lying to his innocent girl, knowing full well that he himself had married and settled down on a ranch, giving up the life of a drifter forever. Whatever had possessed him to accompany O'Sullivan on this outrageous trip, he would never know.

Lisa sniffled and wiped the tears from her eyes. "You are right, Lee," she whimpered. "Sometimes my emotions run away with me. It's just that I haven't been away from my folks for very long. They kicked me out when I was sixteen. I couldn't get a job, and Rosa was the only one who would take me in when I was down. I owe her something, but I can't go on living this life forever. I just want to settle down with a man and have some babies like every other woman. Is that so bad? You were the only man who ever treated me nice here."

"There'll surely be other men, Lisa. You're young yet. Someone will come along that tickles your fancy. There's many a man would give anything to have a woman like you to warm his bed at night. Just give it some time."

Lee took the fragile woman in his arms and kissed her tenderly. He felt pity for the girl and another, deeper emotion that pulled at him to stay with her.

King and the others were probably wondering

what had happened to him. Lee had to get back to the hotel. As far as any of them knew, he was still at the police precinct undergoing a brutal interrogation by Pinker. He was sure his friend O'Sullivan was worried out of his head.

Lee kissed the girl one final time and left the room and the boarding house, saying his goodbyes and making profuse apologies to Rosa. By the time he reached the hotel it was dark and Lee was famished. He hoped King would be able to order a meal for him.

Inside the hotel, it was business as usual. As one of the more luxurious accommodations in New Orleans, the lobby was constantly booming with activity. Men in three-piece suits and ladies in fine evening gowns came and went, hurrying off to parties or dinners, stopping in the great lobby only long enough to check for telegrams or requests a valet. As Lee walked toward the stairway to the second floor, he was hailed by the night porter. As Lee turned to confront the man, a look of recognition crossed the porter's face.

"Oh, it's you," he said. "I see city living hasn't changed you a bit. Pity."

Lee shot him an angry look. "Don't get smart with me, pal. What do you want?"

"Only to tell you that Mr. King has requested that I send you directly to his room should you arrive." The man looked at Lee and sneered.

"I've arrived," Lee answered. "And that's exactly where I was going before you stopped me. Now, get out of my way before I slit you from ear to ear."

"Oh!" the man exclaimed, and hurried back to his post behind the front desk. Lee glared at him until he busied himself rearranging the many keys posted on the board behind the desk, then he climbed the rest of the steps to King's room and pounded on the door with his fist. There was only silence inside. Lee rapped more urgently and a voice came from within. "All right. All right. Be there in a minute." It was Newport who answered the door. He was dressed in a fresh black suit and held a derringer in his hand, aimed directly at Lee's stomach.

"What the hell," Lee snapped, and took a step back. Newport immediately returned the tiny over-and-under to his vest pocket.

"Very sorry, Morgan. Precautions," Newport said simply, and opened the door to allow Lee entry.

"Morgan!" King shouted from somewhere behind Newport's massive chest. "Get in here. Where the blazes have you been?"

Morgan stepped past Newport sideways and the door was shut and latched behind him. "You did request that I oversee the disposal of liquor on the Rachel, didn't you? I've been pouring booze into the Gulf all afternoon." Lee tossed his bag into the corner and approached the table. King and O'Sullivan were seated and O'Sullivan had one of the largest grins Lee had ever seen spread across his face. Beside King there sat one of the most beautiful women Lee had ever seen. She had long, flowing blonde hair that spilled in curls over her shoulders. Her face radiated a glow that showed a freshness he would never see out West. Lee caught himself staring at her as she lifted a watered drink to her lips.

King also noticed Morgan's look. "This is my daughter, Clarissa," King said, gesturing toward the girl. "Clarissa, this gentleman is Lee Morgan. Tim here brought him out here from Idaho to oversee certain . . .er . . . duties once we've reached Panama.''

"Pleased to meet you, Miss," Lee said, tipping a hat that wasn't there.

"Likewise, Mr. Morgan. It's a pleasure to make your acquantance." Clarissa King appraised Lee from head to boot, sizing the man up and trying to figure what to make of the filthy but rugged sight before her.

A woman. King was bringing along a woman, and his daughter, no less. The danger, the threat of disease, crazed jungle savages, and murderous railroad barons; all this and this lunatic King was bringing along his daughter. And just what was she going to do, mend their clothes and ring the dinner bell? Lee suddenly realized just how crazy King was. The whole damn scheme seemed more and more preposterous, and now this. Lee managed to control himself. Hell, if King wanted to get his sweet little daughter killed, it was none of his business. He'd gone this far. He'd might as well stick it out to the bitter end. They were probably all going to end up supper for a school of piranha anyway.

"Clarissa has been studying South American culture in Boston," King was saying, though Lee hardly heard him through his own musings. "She is familiar with several of the Indian tribes in Central America and will act as interpreter. This little trip will serve as reference for a thesis she is writing over the summer."

"This is so exciting," Clarissa said, suddenly. "I just can't wait to get started. I don't believe any woman has ever had an opportunity like this."

Lee rolled his eyes, despite his immediate attraction to the woman. O'Sullivan saw this and knew exactly what Morgan was thinking, but he hoped Morgan wouldn't protest.

"King," Morgan couldn't resist saying, "have you informed your daughter of the dangers involved in this journey? We're not going on a Sunday school picnic, you know." Both King and his daughter frowned at Lee's statement.

"Morgan," King said, "I consider my daughter an expert on Central American affairs, more so than you will ever be. Not only will this be a unique experience for her, but she will be of invaluable assistance to the success of this expedition. She is perfectly aware of the wildlife we will encounter, and equally aware of the hazards of jungle living."

"That's not what I mean, King, and you know it." Lee pounded his fist on the table so hard that everyone in the room jumped.

"What on earth is he talking about, Daddy?" Clarissa questioned, turning eagerly to her father.

"He is referring to some trouble we might have with the railroad operators down there, my dear." King looked harshly at Morgan and probably would have punched him in the face if his daughter had not been present. "Clarissa, why don't you go to your room and try to get a good night's sleep. We're going to have a full day ahead of us tomorrow and I think you should be fully rested. After all, you've been on that train from Boston for days."

"But . . ." Clarissa protested.

"Clarissa, please do as I say. We have much to discuss here, and it may take quite some time. You really should rest," King insisted.

Clarissa King stood and set her drink on the table, never taking her eyes off Morgan. Then she turned and stomped off to her room, slamming the door behind her.

King turned back to Morgan and glared at him with fire in his eyes. "How dare you attempt to frighten my daughter," he said as soon as the door had shut. "That is one aspect of this trip she is not to know of."

"And why the hell not? If she's so goddam valuable to this trip, then why not let her in on everything? And what the hell are you doing bringing a woman along? We're going to have our hands full as it is. Now you expect me to look after a woman who's never lived ten miles from Boston?"

"That, Mr. Morgan, is none of your concern. The fact that she is going and there will be no more argument about it. Now, as I was saying. You will not breathe a word about the railroad situation in Panama. Neither will you mention the incident by the boat this morning. She will learn of it from the crew in good time, I am sure, but I will not have her alarmed before we set sail. Do you understand?"

O'Sullivan thought the two men were going to go at it right then on the hotel room floor, turning a battle of words into a battle of fists. He was surprised when Lee simply nodded his assent and poured himself a drink from the half bottle of whiskey sitting in the center of the table. He downed the shot in one tilt of the glass.

"All right, King," he said. "You win. This is your expedition and you're paying me good money to go along as troubleshooter, even though I was not invited by you. I'll put up with whatever lunacy you can come up with and I'll even keep an eye out for your daughter, but as I told you before, I'm looking out for my own skin first. Do you understand?"

"Understood," King said, pouring himself

another shot of expensive Irish whiskey. "Now that we have that out of the way," King said more cheerfully, "tell us what happened to you this afternoon. I was beginning to think that Pinker spirited you away forever after they dragged you out of that alley this morning. And by the way, I want to thank you for going after that man this afternoon. Catching him sure got Pinker off our backs. I haven't heard a word out of him since this morning." King laughed at his good fortune.

Lee's anger returned in a flash. "Damn you, King. Can't you think of anything but this expedition? Has it occurred to you that an innocent man died this morning—died only because he was standing between you and a clear shot? The brains splattered all over the cab were more likely than not intended to be yours. Have you considered that at all?"

"Yes, I have, Morgan." King was more sober now. "But the fact remains that the man missed and now he is dead, thanks to you." King suddenly heard a sound coming from the bedroom. He walked slowly to the door and opened it in one sweep. His daughter nearly fell face first onto the floor. "No eavesdropping! Back to bed," he commanded gruffly. The girl stomped off again, wordlessly, and King closed the door.

"Now, Mr. Morgan, tell us what happened."

All four men reseated themselves around the table, Lee taking a position directly across from King. Lee retold the story of his pursuit of the sniper and of almost being killed in the alley. O'Sullivan filled in the rest of the events, the arrival of Pinker and his men. Lee being toted off to the infirmary looking half dead. Pinker had questioned almost every man who had witnessed the incident and had come to the conclusion that the sniper was the same man who had killed Wilkins. He had decided to let the case rest, and allow King to finish their loading and get underway without delay.

But there had been no word from Pinker about Lee's fate. Everyone had spent the afternoon wondering whether he was alive or dead. King, O'Sullivan, and Newport had given orders for the day to men on the boat, then retired to the hotel, fearing for their lives.

King shook his head and spread his fingers out over the table. "It looks bad, gentlemen. All the evidence would indicate that someone or perhaps several people have found out about the purpose of this expedition. I expect from here on in we are in for a rough ride. We should all be especially cautious until we set out tomorrow morning. There may be many more out there looking for our heads. Morgan, I'd like you to stay in this room tonight. I don't want my daughter in any danger. You can sleep on the sofa over there," he said, indicating the chaise longue on the other side of the room. Tim, Newport —I would advise you both to make sure your doors and windows are secure. We don't want to have a repeat of last night's incident." O'Sullivan and Newport nodded. Lee noted that Newport had been strangely silent the entire evening. He decided not to comment, assuming that Newport was probably just scared and worried about what he would have to face over the next several weeks or months. He looked even more nervous when King mentioned locking himself in.

Lee turned back to King. "When I was down at the boat this afternoon, things looked pretty shipshape. We should have no trouble getting underway by eight tomorrow. The men seem to be in good spirits, even if a few of them did lose out on a bet."

"What are you talking about, Lee?" King asked.

"Nothing. Forget it. Just a little joke. A poor one at that." Lee's hunger suddenly got the best of him. He was both famished and exhausted. But without something to fill his acid stomach, he would lie awake the entire night. "If you fellows don't mind," he said, "I'm going to head downstairs and try to wrangle some grub in the kitchen. When I get back I'd like to hit the sack immediately. I want to be wide awake when we push off tomorrow. There's no telling what trouble there might be."

"Fine with me," King said. "I'm about ready to turn in, myself."

Lee went downstairs and, after getting the eye from the porter once again, slipped into the kitchen. The cook objected, but when Lee flashed a wad of bills, he was quickly seated before a feast of leftover supper. When he was finished, he slid a couple of dollars under his plate and passed the cook a couple more for some fresh cigars. He then walked back to King's suite. When he arrived, both King and Newport had returned to their rooms. O'Sullivan remained seated at the huge round table looking wearily out the window at the passing gentry on the street. Lee sat beside him and refilled both of their glasses. Lee was full and decided to top off the dinner with a fresh cigar.

O'Sullivan did not look at him, but instead kept his eyes out the window. "You know, Lee," he said, "sometimes I wonder why I ever got into this business. There's sure no money in it, and people just don't appreciate fine photography. To most folks it's a novelty, even today. Almost like a sideshow attraction. I've always considered myself an artist, but sometimes I wonder if it is an art. Folks don't appreciate a photograph unless it's a portrait of someone."

"You chose it as your profession," Lee mused. "You must enjoy doing it or you wouldn't have started in the first place. Someday folks will appreciate what you do. Fact is, I don't know anyone else who does what you do. I admire that in a man, someone who dares to do something that no one else has an interest in. At least you're not some gambler or gunfighter with no place to call home, and no one to call friend. You've got your studio in Boise and enough government work to keep you going."

"I guess you're right, Lee," O'Sullivan said a bit more cheerfully, but still looking out the window. "It's just that I think sometimes how easy life could have been for me. I could have set up shop here in New Orleans—or anywhere else back East, for that matter—and churned out portraits day after day for people willing to pay a pretty penny. I could have been a rich man, and lived a clean, easy life. I often wonder why I didn't do that."

"You and millions of other folks, too, I bet. There ain't many who're ever satisfied with what they're doing. They're always looking for where they went wrong, dwelling on how they could have done better. Look at me, Tim. You don't think I feel the same way? I could have taken over Spade Bit years ago when my daddy died, but I took to the road instead. Sure, I regret it sometimes, but if I hadn't done what I wanted when I wanted, I wouldn't be where I am or know what I do today."

Lee wondered why he was talking like this. The

mood had been solemn ever since he had returned from the kitchen. He expected that it had something to do with the nature of the trip they were about to go on, and the fact that neither of them might come back alive. There was something about reflecting on one's mortality that made a man wonder how he could have lived his life better.

Lee turned to pour himself another drink and noted that he was starting to feel dizzy from the combination of drink and fatigue. Just as he tipped the bottle, O'Sullivan suddenly stood up, knocking over his chair.

"Did you see that?" he whispered loudly, so as not to awaken King and his daughter.

"What?" Lee said, setting the bottle back on the table.

"There was a flash, a bright light," O'Sullivan said. "Looked like it came from the other side of that building there."

Just then there was a loud booming sound that rattled the window. Lee rushed over to look out. Above the two-story building across the street, Lee could see a faint orange glow. To anyone else it might have been mistaken for the city's lights, but Lee recognized the glow of a fire when he saw one.

"An explosion," Lee said.

O'Sullivan looked at him. "Let's go up on the roof. Maybe we can see what's going on from there."

Lee looked back at him as if he were crazy. "I already know what's going on," Lee said excitedly. "That explosion came from the docks. I'll lay odds that someone's set fire to the ship." The two men didn't have to say another word. Lee grabbed his jacket and ran for the door, with O'Sullivan right behind him.

King groggily came out of his room and looked around. "What's all the commotion?" he asked loudly. But by that time Lee and O'Sullivan were already in the lobby, knocking hotel guests out of their way to get to the scene. King stepped back into his room, latched the door, and buried himself in the bedspread.

When Lee and O'Sullivan arrived on the deck, men were running everywhere. The fire seemed to be limited to the dock and the men were frantically pouring bucket after bucket of sea water on the blaze, trying to control it before it reached the boat.

Lee saw that there was a large hole in the pier, indicating that the explosion had been caused by a small bomb that had perhaps been hidden there during the day.

Lee organized the men into a chain. Buckets were filled with sea water and passed hand over hand until they were given to Lee and O'Sullivan, who doused the fire and worked their way back to the source of the explosion. The pier had weakened somewhat from the blaze and the two had to watch their step to keep from breaking through the charred boards and falling into the dark water below. Lee found himself working next to Jim Cook, who wavered as he passed the buckets to Lee, as if the weight were too much for him. Lee guessed the man had been drinking for hours.

"Heh, heh, I ain't seen this much action in years," the man said as he sloshed another bucket toward Lee.

"Shut up and keep 'em coming," Lee said. The blaze was nearly under control. All that was left burning was a small pile of crates which had been piled a few yards from the original blast. The heat was intense as Lee neared the pile, pouring bucket after bucket onto the heap. He wished he had had the time to get the ship's pump operating and rig up a way to spray water onto the fire. The buckets would have to do for now.

"Did you see or hear anyone?" Lee shouted to Cook over the noise of the blaze and the hollering men.

"Didn't see the explosion," Cook answered, "but there was a fellow prowling around the area about a half hour ago."

"Did you get a look at him?" Lee urged.

"Naw, it was way too dark by then. Feller kinda just hung around looking at the boat for a while, then disappeared. I went back inside and didn't think anything else about it."

Lee couldn't believe the man had not at least been suspicious after what had happened that morning. Then he realized again that Cook was drunk, probably not thinking straight. Lee was about to holler at him for being so stupid when he thought better of it. He was going to need all the friends he could get.

"Did you happen to see what he was wearing?" Lee asked, hoping to get a little more information, something he could go on to find the arsonist.

"That was the queer part. The feller was wearing a black suit—vest and everything. I thought it was kinda odd that a man who looked like he had just stepped out of the opera house would be down on the waterfront this time of evening."

"So why didn't you ask him?" Lee asked, his anger rising again.

Before the man could answer, the pile of crates exploded. Flames shot straight into the air, relighting the sky like a Fourth of July fireworks display. The force of the explosion knocked Lee and O'Sullivan off their feet, and Lee plunged into the river delta. Somehow he managed to remain conscious, struggling to reach the surface before his lungs burst. His head broke the surface and he gasped for breath, groping to get a grip on the moorings. By the time he pulled himself out of the water the blaze had died back down. Acrid smoke seared his lungs. Both O'Sullivan and Cook lay unconscious and Lee rushed to his friend's side.

"The fire," O'Sullivan moaned. "Get the fire, Lee!"

Satisfied that O'Sullivan was alive and not seriously hurt, Lee ran over to Cook, who lay spread-eagle on his back with a queer smile on his face. For an instant Lee thought the man was dead, but when he found a pulse, he guessed that the man had been so drunk that he had simply gone limp when the explosion occurred. He didn't detect any broken bones.

The men had reformed the line and were once again combatting the speading blaze, but Lee noticed it was spreading toward O'Sullivan. He again ran to his friend, seeing that he was trying to rise. Lee told him to relax, then hefted the man on his shoulders and moved him safely onto the boat. If they didn't get the fire out soon, it might spread to the ship. Then they could forget about the expedition forever. The government would never agree to fund another such trip, especially after this one had bungled so easily.

Through the smoke and flame, Lee saw a figure standing on the walkway about twenty feet from the edge of the blaze. He squinted and saw that the man wore a dark suit and had his arms folded across his chest. Lee could not make out the man's identity, but the dark suit put him on guard. He eased his way around the fire to get a better view. It was Pinker.

"Noon," he said abruptly, and walked away.

5

Dawn seemed to take forever to arrive. When it did, Lee walked out of the sleeping quarters of the ship and surveyed the pier. There was a huge hole burnt clear through and charred rubbish and ashes were scattered everywhere. The stench nearly made Lee gag. Fortunately, the boat itself was not damaged, although Lee was sure that that had been the arsonist's intended purpose. He couldn't help but wonder if it had been Pinker himself who had set the bomb. It would have been a convenient way to put a stop to the expedition and King would have been forced to go back to Washington with his tail between his legs.

But Pinker's actions were not those of a man who had just committed a crime. Sure, he had been wearing a dark suit, just like Cook had described. But why would he have returned to the pier? To survey the damage he had done? Most likely not.

Pinker's simple, one-word ultimatum led Morgan to believe that the city's officials had tied Pinker's hands. No matter what mayhem was caused, Pinker would just have to put up with it until the deadline the officials had set. If they were not gone by noon, Pinker would surely be back and would have the power to stop the expedition.

Lee returned to the vessel and walked down the iron steps to the galley. There he put on a pot of coffee and sat down to wait for it to boil. He hoped Cook was not too hung over to fix the men a hearty breakfast. They needed some kind of reward for all the work they had done putting out the fire. It was not under control until nearly midnight and even then a couple of men were forced to sit up the entire night to keep watch.

With the coffee done, Lee sat back to enjoy a cup. He sipped it hot and black, not even bothering to filter out the grounds. Through the wall to his back, he could hear men stirring and he guessed the smell of the coffee had awakened them. It was nearly seven before the men were all up and at work. Lee expected that King and the others would be showing up very soon, King probably furious at being left unguarded.

Taking his tin cup with him, Lee returned to the sleeping quarters where O'Sullivan was beginning to stir. Lee threw the blanket off the man. "Up and at 'em, you lazy bum," Lee said, laughing.

The still groggy man opened one eye to see who was disturbing him, then shut it as if to go back to sleep. "Oh, Lee, it's only you. I was just trying to get up. Help me out of bed, will you?" The man was so tired he could hardly speak.

"Like hell I will," Lee said. "You're not getting out of that bunk till I say so. Doc gave you enough sedatives to put my best stallion out for a week."

"Where am I? What happened?" O'Sullivan insisted, trying to prop himself up onto his elbows.

Lee pushed him back down, feeling badly that he had joked with the ailing man when he came in. He hadn't realized how sick he still was. "You're on the Rachel," Lee said. "There was another explosion last night and it knocked you for a loop. You got a few burns and went into shock. Doc and I brought you down here. I've been with you all night. Doc says you'll be all right in a day or two. In the meantime, just rest. And don't get up whatever you do. I don't want you stumbling around above deck."

O'Sullivan opened his mouth to respond but only a gurgle came out, and he fell asleep again immediately. Lee pulled the covers up around the man's neck and left the room when he started snoring.

Lee considered going to see what had happened to King, but thought better of it. The man could fend for himself during the walk to the pier. Lee felt certain King wouldn't want to get into a cab again for a good long time. He stopped in the captain's cabin to get better acquainted with the man he had met only briefly the night before.

"I want to thank you, Morgan, for saving my ship," Captain Johnson was saying. "If it hadn't been for you coming along when you did, she would have burned for sure. Those boys King hired don't know any more about putting out a fire than they do about sailing. I'll wager half of them have never been on a boat in their lives."

Lee was also sure that was the case, but he knew King hadn't hired the men for their naval abilities. Their real test would come once they reached the steaming jungles of Panama. Lee asked the captain for a tour of the engine room. He didn't know any more about oceangoing ships than the rest of the men aboard, but there was no reason to let the captain think otherwise. When they emerged into sunlight again, King, Newport and Clarissa were standing on the pier inspecting the damage. The group of men that had been charged with cleaning duty on the deck were standing in a circle around them, gesturing wildly, and probably filling King in on every detail. When he saw Lee and the captain standing on deck looking at the group, he strode quickly over, knocking several of the crewmen out of the way.

"Captain," he whispered. "we are to leave immediately. There will be no further delay. I intend to see that there are no more incidents of this nature. If we are out at sea, that will be most unlikely. Get those boilers going, have your crew pull in the mooring lines and shove off. Morgan, I want to have a word with you—in private. Meet me in the stateroom. I'll be with you in just a moment."

Both Lee and the captain left immediately and King returned to the group on the pier. "We are leaving immediately. Please, everyone get on board and prepare to shove off. Newport, would you mind giving Clarissa a brief tour of the ship? She should be able to find her way around. When you are finished, take her to my quarters and show her where she can change into more suitable clothes. That pink dress is apt to give some of the scum on this ship the wrong idea."

Newport let a smile break through his usually stony face. "Yes, sir. Consider it done."

"Good," King said. "I'll be down shortly. I first have some business to attend to up here."

Newport and Clarissa disappeared below deck and King looked after the two for several moments after they were gone. He wondered if Morgan might not be right. This was no place for a budding young lady, especially one so naive and unworldly. Still, she had insisted upon coming, even going so far as to take a train to New Orleans against his orders. She had even managed to get a government escort by claiming that King was expecting her. How could he send her back?

King watched anxiously while the crew pulled in the gangplank and breathed a sigh of relief when the ship finally shuddered and moved away from the dock. Perhaps on the open water, they could get away from whoever was trying to intimidate them, and away from Pinker's prying eyes. Perhaps there would be no trouble at all in Panama. However, at this point, King could do nothing but cross his fingers.

He stepped through the hatch, and because of his bulky frame, practically had to walk sideways through the corridor. When he entered the stateroom, Lee was sitting alone at the solitary table, drinking his second cup of coffee and looking over a map of the province of Panama. He looked leaner than the night before and King guessed that he had removed the bulky bandages encasing his chest. As King entered the room, Lee pulled out one of the Cuban cigars he had managed to purchase from the cook in the hotel the night before. He struck a wooden match on the underside of the table and lit up, taking short little puffs and twirling the cigar to get an even light.

"What's on your mind," Lee said, blowing a ring of smoke in King's direction.

"You know very well what is on my mind. You left your post last night. If we had been attacked, my daughter could have been hurt. My suite was left unguarded."

"You mean *you* could have been hurt, don't you?" Lee asked. "You saw the remains of the pier. Someone planted a bomb. From what I can see, you are more concerned about this ship's safety than that of your daughter. I simply opted for the path you yourself would have taken."

King's eyes burned and his chubby face turned a deep red. "Why, you stinking scum. I'll . . ."

"Ah, ah," said Morgan, laying his Colt on the table. "Watch your step. We may be away from Pinker and his men, but I can still argue self-defense. Now, about those men you promised me . . ."

King looked sullen and slumped into the seat across from Lee. "What of them?" he asked. He knew he was going to have to let Morgan have his way to a certain extent, but he'd be damned if he was going to let him take over the ship. King was still in charge of the expedition, and would demand that Morgan be set adrift in a lifeboat if the situation got too out of hand. The captain would have no choice. He had been commanded by the federal authorities to follow King's wishes unless the ship was in danger.

"I want ten of my choosing, and I guarantee you they will be the best you have. You can use them any way you want now. But once on shore, they will be strictly under my command. They can carry out their other duties in shifts. But I want at least five men under me at any given moment. You can retain your leadership over this expedition, but if there's trouble—and you ought to know damn well by now that there's going to be trouble—we are going to need a force to defend the party. Are we agreed on this matter?"

"No, we are not agreed. There will be no trouble. Colombia has given their permission for this expedition and I am assured that the governor of the province is quite anxious to help us in any way. But it would seem I have no choice in the matter," King said, nodding toward Lee's pistol still lying on the table. "You will have your men."

King quickly changed the subject. "By the way. Where is O'Sullivan? I haven't seen him since I arrived. He did make it on board, didn't he?"

"He's down in the sleeping quarters," Lee answered. "Got a few burns in the fire last night. Doc thought it would be best to keep him knocked out for a couple of days."

"Hurt bad?" King suddenly looked concerned.

"Just a few scratches and burns. He hit his head pretty hard when that pile blew. I still don't know what it was. But do you really care?"

King looked peeved. "Of course I care what happens to Tim. We've known each other far longer than you and he have. We've had a lot of good times together—some bad ones, too. This isn't the first undertaking of this nature we've been on." King found himself wishing he had a stiff drink, but he knew there was none on board. "Look, Morgan," he said. "We have our differences, I know. We both have our own ideas about how to go about getting things done. But that's no reason for us to not be friends. You've got your men, but I've got my duty. The United States Government is depending on me to get the information we uncover safely back to Washington. What do you say we call this little feud of ours even and get on with the business at hand?"

"Fine by me," Lee said. "But when trouble comes, I'm the one giving the orders. I'll not see innocent men killed because of you."

Later in the afternoon, after the ship followed the river to the sea and land was no longer in sight, Lee called Cook to look after O'Sullivan while he stepped out for some fresh air. Cook was still hung over from his drinking bout and Lee thought he looked almost as ill as O'Sullivan. Cook, however, insisted he was all right, so Lee left the two men and went above. O'Sullivan had remained unconscious most of the day, only occasionally awakening to question where he was. Lee had assured him he was all right and made sure to change the dressing on his burns frequently, just like the doctor ordered.

Once on the bow, Lee took several breaths of fresh sea air. He hadn't been out on open water for some time. In fact, the closest he had been to water for the last year had been his Saturday bath. The mist felt good against his skin, almost like a fine rain.

He was watching the gulls circling the ship. They were not yet far enough out to sea for them to return to shore. As he stared, he felt a presence behind him.

He turned to see a young man dressed in jeans and flannel shirt.

"Howdy," he said, turning back to the birds. "Fine day for sailing, ain't it?"

"Yes, it is, isn't it," came the reply.

Lee turned around again, puzzled. Then he saw that the young man was really Clarissa King. Without her makeup and fancy clothes, she could have passed easily for one of the younger men aboard ship.

"Sorry, Miss, I didn't mean to be discourteous. I thought you was one of the boys."

"Well!" Clarissa exclaimed. "That's a fine thing for a gentleman to say to a lady."

"I didn't mean nothing by it, Miss. I only got a glimpse of you. Your clothes didn't help matters none."

Clarissa was obviously irritated. "A gentleman should always recognize a lady when he sees one, no matter what her attire."

Lee chuckled. "Ain't too many men would recognize you as a lady right now without your speaking first. Least not in that getup."

"And just what is wrong with this getup, as you call it? It is perfectly appropriate for wearing aboard ship."

Lee was getting nowhere. He had started this encounter off on the wrong foot and things were quickly going downhill. He spent most of his time at odds with King. He certainly didn't want to generate bad feelings with his daughter as well. "I apologize, Miss," he said. "For the kind of trip we're going on, those duds will do just fine."

Clarissa's mood lightened as she saw that she was

going to have her way with the man her father was having such a hard time handling. "Apology accepted," she said simply. She walked over to stand beside Lee and both leaned over the railing to look into the ocean as the water sped past. Lee couldn't help but admire her looks, even through the baggy pants and loose-fitting shirt. She had the face of a child and the disposition of a woman who would not be manipulated.

"Mr. Morgan . . . or may I call you Lee?" she said at length.

Lee took this question as a sign of friendship. "Be my guest," he said.

"Lee," she continued, "I must tell you that my father has asked me to stay away from you. He said not to even speak to you if I could help it. I'm inclined to believe he doesn't trust you around me."

"I can't imagine why he wouldn't," Lee said, wondering what she was getting at.

Clarissa continued, "After we left New Orleans, he took me aside and told me all about the problem we might be having with those awful railroad people. He even told me about the trouble you had back in the city—the shootings and such. I asked him about the fire and he seemed to think that was related, too. He said he had hired you to look out after us. Did he leave anything out, Lee?"

"I reckon not," Lee said. "Sounds like he filled you in on everything."

"Then why is it that he doesn't trust you? You seem like an honest man. It sounds to me like you're here to protect us. I just don't understand why he dislikes you so."

"It's 'cause my idea of protecting you folks goes

against his interest in Panama. He started out thinkin' this was going to be one big party. I guess he was hoping to get a medal for himself or something. But I think he's starting to see the danger we're up against. Those rail barons he told you about are a ruthless bunch—both in Central America and in the States. All they're concerned with is making money, and they don't care a whit who they have to hurt to get it. And that includes pretty girls like you. They have hundreds of bandits and Indians at their disposal, paid to do anything they ask. And if they plan to come after us, we don't stand a chance unless we are prepared to fight. That's the part your father doesn't understand. I hope you'll help me make him see that."

Clarissa moved a bit closer to Lee. Their arms touched and Lee backed away. "I understand, Lee. Sometimes my father can get a little carried away with his plans. He'll come to his senses once he sees what Panama is really like."

"You talk as if you know," Lee said.

"Only through books," Clarissa said. "I've been interested in that part of the world since I was in second grade. One of my teachers once gave me a book with drawings of Mayan culture. The Mayans disappeared hundreds of years ago. No one really knows what happened to their civilization. They say it was almost as advanced as most of those in Europe at one time. But there're still thousands of Indians down there. I want to learn even more about them, and first-hand experience is about the best way I know of."

"That's very noble," Lee said, "but also very dangerous. I guess you know now what you're getting into."

Clarissa looked into his eyes ominously. "I sincerely hope you are wrong about the dangerous part, Lee. It's getting a bit chilly out here. I think I should go back to daddy's quarters. He's probably wondering where I am by now."

"I'll walk you back," Lee said. "It's about time I checked on O'Sullivan. That old coot I left him with has probably dozed off."

"I would like that very much, Lee. But I think I'd better go back alone. Daddy said I musn't speak to you and I think it's best that he think I'm following his orders for now. I hope to see you again soon."

Clarissa walked back inside, huddling her arms around her against the sea breeze. Lee followed not far behind her, restraining himself to keep his distance. He might never understand King, but it was certain that he understood that this young woman was attracted to him.

Back in his sleeping quarters, Lee arrived to find Cook slumped in a chair and snoring loudly. Bending over the man, Lee smelled whiskey on the cook's breath but he could find no bottle in the room. The old fellow hides 'em better than anyone else aboard, Lee thought. Lee woke the man and in jest threatened to throw him into the ocean. Cook wasn't quite sure whether Lee was serious or not. After putting a good scare into him, Lee sent the man on his way. It was getting on in the afternoon and the man still had to prepare supper for forty people.

Lee changed the dressing on O'Sullivan's wounds without waking him, then tended to his own. Neither was very deep and had scabbed over nicely.

The night before he had removed his bandages and the air seemed to be doing wonders for the gashes. Lee applied a little dab of O'Sullivan's dressing and rubbed it into the wounds until it disappeared. Then he replaced his shirt and settled into the chair for a nap.

At dinner he avoided sitting with King, Newport, and Clarissa, preferring to chat with the captain once again. The captain was a jolly sort of fellow, with a smile that never left his face. He told Lee dozens of sea stories—some more than once, but Lee was polite enough to listen again and Lee told him of his adventures and women out West. The captain was particularly rapt as Lee told of striking it rich in the Yukon, a place the captain had often heard stories about. He had never heard of anyone actually hitting a lode big enough to brag about.

Captain Johnson had served the South during the war. He was in charge of a division in New Orleans charged with protecting the mouth of the Mississippi. After the war he had captained huge paddlewheels up and down the Mississippi as far north as the Ohio. It was a lucrative business, but he had had the misfortune to have one of his boilers blow, setting off an explosion that killed several passengers. The company that owned the steamboat claimed the captain had been negligent and theatened legal action. He disappeared for a couple of years, drifting back East and working in the Brooklyn Navy Yard, eventually saving enough money to purchase the ancient steamer they were riding in.

Although Lee listened to Johnson's stories with great interest, he couldn't help but notice that

Clarissa King had been staring at him throughout the meal. King had been looking his way, too. Lee decided to ignore them both and return to his quarters without saying a word to either. He had nothing more to say to King, and if he acknowledged Clarissa, King might begin to suspect something and cause more trouble than he already had.

Back in his cabin, O'Sullivan was lying drowsily awake in the dim light. The ship, though old, was equipped with an electric generator which supplied the necessary power for lighting, and Lee was glad he had remembered to leave the light on in case his friend awakened.

"Hello, Lee," O'Sullivan said. "I've been waiting up for you."

Lee sat beside his old friend. "Somebody ought to take a picture of you, Tim. You're really a sight."

"Thanks for the encouragement, pal. How long have I been out? Feels like a month." O'Sullivan rubbed his head and closed his eyes again.

"Since last night," Lee said. "How're you feeling?"

"Like I've been wrestling bulls and swimming in acid. Doc think I'll live?"

"At least another twenty years," Lee said, smiling. "I was getting worried about you, pard. Doc put you out for a good long time. Why don't you try to get another night of shut-eye. I'll get Doc in to look you over in the morning. You shouldn't get out of bed until then."

"Don't think I could if I wanted to," O'Sullivan said. "I'll just lay here and agonize another night, if you don't mind."

O'Sullivan was silent after this last statement and

Lee readied himself for bed. Within minutes of turning out the light, he was fast asleep, dreaming of wild horses running.

"We're going down! We're going down!" O'Sullivan was screaming. Lee awoke suddenly, thinking O'Sullivan was delirious. As he got up to turn on the light, Lee was thrown across the cabin and into the counter against the wall. The ship gave another lurch and O'Sullivan fell out of bed and rolled across the floor in agony. Lee tumbled on top of him, but soon regained his footing. He finally reached the light and saw that the cabin was a shambles. O'Sullivan was definitely not delirious, and the ship could very well be going down. Lee had no idea what was happening.

He managed to make it to the door. Once in the corridor, he was nearly trampled by men running from one end of the ship to the other. He corralled one of them, grabbing him by the collar.

"What the hell's going on?" Lee shouted. "Did we hit something?"

The ship gave another lurch, sending the two men against the wall. The crewman pulled loose of Morgan. "We've run into a squall. The wind started kicking up about an hour ago. Looks like we're in the thick of it right now. It ain't a bad storm, but we're taking on water, and the pumps won't start!"

Lee waved the man on and climbed to the bridge. Johnson and his first mate, Wilson Davies, were there trying to keep the ship on course against the wind and the waves. The young first mate was panicky. Fear was etched into his pale face. The young man was probably on the open sea for the first time.

Lee saw that the captain was trying to calm him, while frantically working the ship's controls. Lee stepped in just as the ship was tossed by another massive wave.

"Anything I can do?" Lee shouted.

"Not . . . up here," the captain said, almost as if Lee were not there. He had enough on his hands without worrying about some cowboy getting in his way. "Get down to the hold and see if you can get the pumps started. We've taken on a good deal of water. If it gets to the engine room, we're not going to be going anywhere." Just then, the lights went out and the ship slipped into darkness.

Lee picked up a couple of candles and went below. In the hold, the men had stopped trying to get the pumps started. Without electricity, it was hopeless. Without stopping to survey the scene, Lee sent two men out to round up as many as they could to man the manual pumps. While they were gone, Lee and the others got the pumps operating. Then he set out for the engine room. As he stepped in, water reached his ankles. He began to set up the pumps there and was going back for help when the engines stopped altogether.

Lee looked at the engineer, who threw up his hands in frustration. "Too much water," he said. "There's nothing I can do now, least not till she dries out."

Lee noticed the water had stopped coming in. And the heavy jolts he felt just moments before had stopped. The ship just seemed to roll and sway, almost back to normal.

Lee indicated for the engineer to get a few men to

help him pump the room out and clean up the mess the storm had left in its wake.

Back on the bridge, the captain was sitting with his head between crossed arms. The first mate was weeping silently in one corner of the cabin. Lee entered and shook the captain, who looked dejected and frustrated.

"The engines are down," he said. "We're dead in the water until they can be started again. Have you heard anything from the engine room?"

Lee looked out at the clearing sky. "I've got men down there pumping it out now. Engineer doesn't seem to think there's any serious damage. The cold water probably stopped the boilers."

"At least the storm's blown over," the captain said. "I've been through a lot worse, but that one was pretty bad for this time of year. It ain't yet hurricane season, but you never can tell what you're going to run into in these waters. There's probably been more ships sunk in the Gulf than all of the Atlantic."

"Your boy looks like he's taking it pretty hard. Is he hurt bad?" Lee asked.

"Damn fool ain't hurt at all," Johnson answered. "Told me in New Orleans he's had experience at sea. That's the last time I ever trust a fast-talking whippersnapper. Damn coward could have got us all killed."

"Aw, don't be so hard on him," Lee said. "We're all right and the ship's still floating."

Obviously Lee didn't know the Navy's penalties for a crew member deserting his post. The captain looked at Lee and decided he wasn't a sailing man after all.

"I'm going to check on my friend, O'Sullivan. Why don't you send that boy down to see Doc," he said. "He looks pretty shook up."

Lee left the bridge and went back to his cabin. O'Sullivan had climbed back into his bed and was sitting on the edge with his knees propped up under his chin. He looked almost in shock again.

Lee poured him a glass of water. "Drink this," he said. "You all right?"

O'Sullivan shakily took the glass and took a sip to wet his lips. He hadn't had anything to eat or drink since his accident. "I . . . You must think I'm a damn fool, Lee," he said. "Waking up screaming like that, I mean. Is the ship okay?"

"I wouldn't be sitting here jawing with you if it weren't. And don't think you're a fool. You're still delirious from the doctor's dope."

"I don't hear the engines any more," O'Sullivan said sullenly, still looking straight ahead.

"They've stopped on us," Lee said. "The engineer's promised to have 'em going again as soon as we can get the place pumped out. The storm's passed over us and there's no danger of sinking. So why don't you just lay back down and get some more shut-eye. It'll be morning soon and I'll send Doc down to look you over. He's probably got his hands full right now."

O'Sullivan didn't say another word, but lay back and closed his eyes. Lee was starting to feel bad for him. The man had already been through hell and they weren't even close to Panama. God only knew what would have become of the man if Lee hadn't decided to accompany him.

Although Lee was not so concerned with King, he

decided to check in on him and Clarissa to make sure they were unharmed. Besides, it would give him a good excuse to visit with the woman, though he would have to be careful not to mention their conversation the day before.

In front of their cabin, Lee pounded on the door. There was no response. Lee tried the knob but found that it was locked from the inside. He pounded with his fist again. "Come on, open up in there," he hollered.

There was still no answer and Lee began to worry. What if they were injured, or worse. He would have to get a crowbar to pry the door open. But just as he turned, he heard the latch move. Turning back, he heard someone fumbling with the knob and then the door opened a crack. It opened wider and Clarissa King fell out into Lee's strong arms. Lee lifted her and carried her back into the chamber. The room was blacker than night and Lee had to struggle to find her bunk while she was in his arms. He stumbled over something on the floor. A box, he assumed. After Clarissa had been stretched out on her bed, Lee pulled a candle out of his pocket and lit it with one of the few dry matches he had left. He gently shook Clarissa and she immediately opened her eyes.

"Daddy," she said. "Where is he?"

Lee looked into her pleading eyes. He certainly had to admire this girl. No sooner was she conscious than she was worrying about her father. With his hand gently covering her face, Lee shut the girl's eyes again. "Sleep now," he said. "I'll find him. I guarantee it."

Lee stood and turned to survey the room. He immediately stepped back in shock. There on the floor, instead of a box, was King, a large gash across his forehead. Blood matted his hair. He was unconscious and still bleeding. Lee ran to the corridor leading to the room and grabbed the first man he saw.

"Give me a hand," Lee said. "There's a man been hurt bad in here."

Inside the room, the two men struggled to lift the heavy body. Lee had to move the massive bookshelf that had fallen on King. The thing had probably toppled away from the wall and hit him squarely across the head. The two men managed to drag King to the corridor where others joined them. Together they hauled him off to the infirmary. Lee stayed behind to wait for the doctor's report.

"How is he?" Morgan asked after the doctor had examined King.

"He would seem to be normal for a middle-aged man. His pulse is regular. I didn't detect any broken bones. There's just the cut on his forehead, and of course there will be quite a bruise. But I see no reason for him not to regain consciousness in a few hours. He ought to be as good as new by tomorrow. How's his daughter? Was she hurt?"

"Naw. She just passed out from all the excitement, I reckon. I'm going back to check on her now."

As much as he disliked King, he was glad the man was not seriously hurt. If for no reason but Clarissa's sake. It was going to be enough of a shock for her to learn that her father was in the infirmary. Lee hoped he could keep her calm. He knew that, in spite of the image she tried to project, Clarissa had a fragile disposition. The death of her father might have been a shock too great for her to bear.

Back in King's cabin, the candle had burned itself out and Lee lit another before entering the room. The girl had not moved since Lee had left. Lee soaked a cloth with cool water and began to wipe her face, hoping to awaken and comfort her.

She remained asleep and he pulled a chair up beside her. The crew bailing out the engine room would just have to do without him. Tending to Clarissa was more important at the moment. Lee leaned back and stretched out his legs. Just as the soft chair and the rolling of the boat in the current was about to put him to sleep, Clarissa awakened.

"Lee Morgan," she said, not a little surprised. "What are you doing here? Where's daddy?" The girl had forgotten about the storm and couldn't figure out why Lee was sitting in her room, sleeping in her father's chair, no less.

"Don't you remember?" Lee asked.

"I don't know," Clarissa said. "We hit a bump of something and the bookshelf fell on top of daddy when he tried to get up to see what was happening. Then the lights went out and . . . I don't remember anything else. Is everything okay?"

"There was a storm," Lee said, moving to the edge of the chair. "You must have passed out as soon as the lights went out." Clarissa tried to sit, but Lee pushed her back onto the bunk. "Lay back down there. I have some bad news to tell you."

"Bad news! What do you mean? Where's daddy?" she demanded.

"That's just it. Your father's been hurt. Got a nasty cut on his head when the shelf fell on him. It was a good thing you pulled yourself together long enough to let me in. No tellin' what might have happened if you hadn't."

"Oh, my God!" Clarissa gasped and threw her hand to her mouth when she realized what had actually happened. "Where is he? I want to see him, Lee. Right now!"

"He's in the infirmary," Lee said coldly. "Doc's taking good care of him. I'm afraid you can't see him now, though. He's unconscious and you're much to weak to be walking around."

"I am not," she insisted, struggling to get out of the bunk. "Now, if you will excuse me . . ."

Lee blocked her from rising and she moved to go around him. He clasped her wrists in his strong hands and held her in place, realizing he had never been so close to her. Her hands felt soft and tender. Struggling to get away from his grip, she found herself being drawn even closer to him. Her face was just inches from his and he could smell the sweet perfume that excited him at their meeting above deck. Suddenly, she stopped resisting. Lee released his hold on her and placed his arms around her tiny waist, inching closer to her lovely lips with every sway of the ship.

Clarissa broke from the stare that was drawing her in. Though she wanted him badly, this was neither the time nor the place. She hit him hard in the chest with both of her hands. Lee was caught off guard and reeled back slightly. Clarissa brought up her hand and slapped him soundly across the cheek.

"You will keep your hands off me in the future, Lee Morgan," she said bluntly. "I am a respectable lady, not some barroom floozy who lets just any man have his way with her. My concern at the moment is for my father, so you will please leave these quarters and allow me to see him."

Lee stared at her, wondering whether to smack her back or laugh. The girl was certainly a fighter. Her will was equally as strong as her father's. Though his desire for her was great, he knew better than to push the matter. Right now he needed an ally more than a lover.

"Sorry," he said. "Don't know what could have come over me." Lee chuckled at his own sarcasm. "If you want to head over to the infirmary, be my guest. But don't come calling on me when you collapse on the floor."

Lee rose and left the room, leaving a very confused Clarissa behind.

Days passed. The engineer had gotten the engine running again after the storm. They had drifted some miles off course, but under the captain's skillful hands, they had managed to make up the lost time in a day. King's men were growing restless. None of them had spent much time aboard a ship and that fact was the cause of many a fight. However, considering the tension they were all feeling, Lee was surprised that there had not been much more trouble.

King regained consciousness the day after the storm. Clarissa had gone to the infirmary after Lee left, but the doctor had refused to let her see her father. She had begged and cried and threatened, but the doctor stood firm.

Lee had spoken privately to King only once since the storm, and determined that the accident had only served to make him more stubborn than before.

Then there had been the big meeting when King had finally revealed exactly where they were going and what was the nature of their expedition. None of the crew was surprised, since most had taken a peek at the carefully packed equipment in the hold. The flooding had given them ample opportunity to examine anything they liked.

O'Sullivan also recovered nicely, although he tossed and turned in his bunk every night because his burns itched so badly. O'Sullivan and Morgan had been standing on the ship's prow catching the breeze and watching the waves slap against the bow when land was first sighted.

There had been no further confrontation with Clarissa. Lee stayed out of her way. He found himself desiring her more each day, but noticed that most of the men aboard ship were demonstrating the same affection for her. He attributed it to the long ocean journey. Though she rarely spoke to him, Lee felt that she was still playing havoc with his affections. She would flirt with him one day and the next not even look his way at mealtime. Lee decided to let things fall where they would. He would show no interest in the woman whatsoever, no matter what he was feeling.

"Well, there it is," O'Sullivan said. "I feel like a damn Spanish conquistador seeing it for the first time. We might as well be. There isn't one of us who knows what to expect when we arrive."

"King still thinks this is going to be a picnic," Lee said. "I know just what to expect. Pure hell for days on end. That is, if we don't rile up the natives and get ourselves killed first. It's only about fifty miles across the isthmus, but if I know King, we're going to be chased every step of the way. No telling what kind of arrangements have been made with the Colombians."

"Or if any really have been made," O'Sullivan observed.

Lee didn't like the sound of the burly Irishman's last statement. He knew all too well it could be true.

Lee opted to change the subject. "Tim, have you ever been to Central America before?"

"I've been on shoots in Mexico. Beautiful country. But never this far south. I'm getting anxious about photographing Panama. I hear it's like another world. Unspoiled, jungles, Indians that ain't never seen a white man, all manner of exotic creatures. I could spend a year down here and still probably not get enough shots."

"You mean the kind of creatures that are gonna have us for supper the first night we're there?"

"You don't know the half of it, Lee. I've been reading up on this place ever since King first mentioned the trip to me last year. Pulled just about every book I could find out of the Boise library. Rail barons and jungle Indians ain't half of our worries. Even without other human beings, the place is treacherous enough. Half the country is swamp and the other half jungle. White men pick up malaria and cholera faster than a cold back home. You got to keep yourself covered night and day. Otherwise the mosquitos will carry you off. There was this one fellow who spent a year there researching the Indians who wrote that he'd seen the buggers so thick that their burned bodies put out a candle. Damn things coat Lake Gatun like a thick fog.

"Then there's the snakes: fer-de-lance, bush-masters. Things are worse than rattlers. Least with rattlers you can hear them. These things wait in trees and drop on you as you pass under. Deadliest things there ever were. You ever seen a coral snake, Lee? Pretty little things. Look like tattooed worms. But one bite and you're dead in five minutes. If there's an antidote, only the Indians know about it. Ain't never been a white man bit and lived to tell about it."

Lee was dumbfounded. He couldn't believe people would actually pay to cross such a hellhole, no matter how much gold and silver there was in California.

"If it's so bad," he asked, "how'd they ever get a railroad built across it? Hardly sounds worth the effort."

"If you gauge worth in terms of human life, it wasn't. But all the rail men are after is money. And they have plenty of it down here, too. When the line across Panama was first started, they used Indian labor. But there weren't enough to do all the work. They brought in thousands of folks from the West Indies to wallow in the mire and put in track. Disease cut 'em down faster than a Gatling gun. Mosquitos just ate 'em alive. They got the work done, all right, but the workers' bodies had to be carried out by the wagonload, while the railroads reaped the profits."

"And now the United States Government is planning to do the very same thing all over again," Lee observed. "Makes you wonder if they ain't any better than the rail barons."

"That's about the size of it, though the government's reasons aren't purely for profit. There's a lot more folks going west now than twenty years ago, and the government feels obliged to help them get there. Right now there's a lot of folks been crossing via Nicaragua. Fact is, that's the government's first choice for the canal site. Half the country is one big lake and there ain't much overland travel involved. Washington's on much better terms with the Nicaraguan government, but who knows, a hundred years from now, we might be at war with them. Right now, things are running smoothly. An American named William Walker was once the president of the country."

"An American?" Lee asked, shocked to hear this news.

"For a while," O'Sullivan said. "He was pretty much the puppet of the company running the route across the country. Sat fat and happy in his office until he started to believe he really was in charge. He got out of line and the company had him thrown out of the country. When he tried to come back the company arranged to have him shot."

"That's almost unbelievable," said Lee.

"Well, it's the truth. It just goes to show you how greedy folks are down here and what they'll do to preserve what control they have. The Indians don't give them no trouble. They give them jobs and pay them more than they've ever seen in their lives. Which is just a step above nothing, I might add."

"And there's the same kind of situation in Panama?" Lee asked.

"Similar, but not exactly. You see, Panama is merely a province of Colombia, and Colombia maintains much more independence than Nicaragua.

They keep pretty close tabs on the railroad. As I was saying before, the U.S. Government thinks Panama is a prime spot for the canal. Lake Gatun almost splits the country in half and there are only a few miles of land connecting the two bodies of water. Thousands more will have to be brought in to build it, and the working conditions will be much worse than when the railroad was built, despite the plentiful supplies of quinine. But Washington thinks the effort will be worth the price. More people will be able to move west and for a cheaper price."

"And the railroads don't want to contend with the competition," Lee put in.

"Exactly," O'Sullivan said. "Aside from that, the government wants to be able to move the fleet from one ocean to the other quickly and easily. As I told you on the train, war's bound to come sooner or later and the government wants to be prepared."

Lee mulled over this for a while, watching the mouth of the bay come closer. It was a beautiful sunny day and the water was a brilliant blue. In the distance, over the shore, thin, wispy clouds rushed by on their way elsewhere. It seemed a very unlikely place for trouble to develop. Almost like paradise.

Lee broke out of his reverie and again questioned O'Sullivan. "So what's our agenda? Has King got this whole thing planned out or are we going to play it by ear?"

"King will most likely explain everything once we're on shore. I guess he doesn't want to divulge any more information until he has to. But I can give you a quick idea of how the expedition is likely to go."

"I'd appreciate it," Lee said.

"Well, we'll probably land in Cristobal within the hour. Supposedly, there will be representatives from the Panamanian provincial government there to meet us. Colombia has made arrangements for us to spend the night there. In the morning we head overland to Lake Gatun, where King should begin to set up his surveying team. Once he's done, or while he's working, rather, the rest of us will build rafts so we can make the trek across the lake. And it is one huge lake. King will want to spend at least a couple of days taking measurements of the tide and water depth. Once that's done, we go overland through about twenty miles of dense jungle and flatlands and arrive in Balboa where we should have a ship waiting for us. That will take us back up the coast to Nicaragua, where we will reverse the route taken by most of the settlers."

"Where are we most likely to run into trouble?" Lee wanted to know. And they rounded the bend and saw Cristobal looming ahead.

"Most likely not until we reach the stretch toward Balboa. It's there that we will be working almost parallel with the railroad. If anyone knows we're coming that's where they'll come gunning for us."

Lee was somewhat relieved. At least they were going to have a few days of relative comfort.

But that was before he saw the battalion of men with rifles and cannons waiting for them on the town's only wharf.

6

Esteban de Narvez was a man of small stature. He was of Spanish descent but always made it a point to cover up the fact that he had a touch of Indian blood. Though shorter than most men, he compensated for it by looking as fierce as possible at all times. His thick black hair was unruly, he went unshaven for days at a time, and he wore a thick oily moustache which, when wet, drooped well below his chin.

He spoke English well, and like many of his other countrymen, considered himself a patriot. He had been raised in Colombia, though born in the city of Panama, and had always thought of Panama as home. Colombia had sent him to his homeland after his graduation from the university, and he had served his country so well that they had made him governor of the province six months before. That had lasted until two weeks ago. It was then that he learned of the King expedition and what it could mean for him. He immediately took over the military and proclaimed Panama's secession from Colombia.

He declared himself president as two dozen men had done before him. The others had failed to keep Colombia from halting their revolution. But Narvez would not fail. He now had something the others did not: two American interests competing for his new country.

As the Rachel sailed through the San Blas islands and into the bay, he had positioned his soldiers so as to intercept the boat. He wanted a word with this man King, this man who would build a canal through his country.

Aboard the ship, no one knew what was going on. Men were scattering all over the deck. The captain sent his first mate below to get King. O'Sullivan and Lee just stared mutely from the prow where they had been talking. Narvez's men were lined up all along the wharf, their rifles shouldered and ready to fire.

One of Narvez's newly appointed generals was giving the commands. "Captain," he shouted through cupped hands. "You will tie up here and your crew will come ashore immediately. All of them!"

Johnson steered the steamer to the dock and several of his crew threw the mooring lines to the soldiers who were waiting to retrieve them. Johnson's crew eyed the soldiers warily, hoping not to make a move that would cause the men to start shooting. They also hoped they weren't about to lose their ship, their only way back to the States, but for the moment, they were more concerned with the preserving of their lives.

"You will leave your weapons on board. They will not be molested," the general was shouting. "Every man will come ashore at once. Captain, you may remain with your ship if you wish. Any man bringing a weapon ashore will be shot without question. Is that understood?"

The men began to file down the gangplank, leaving their guns and knives where they stood. As the last crewman stepped ashore and lined up along the wharf, King and Clarissa arrived on deck. Lee and O'Sullivan quickly joined them.

"What's going on here?" King blustered. "Why have you stopped this vessel? We are here on orders of the Government of the United States, under agreement of Colombia and Governor Narvez!"

Lee turned on him, hoping to keep King from getting himself shot. "Shut up, you blustering asshole, and get down there if you don't want your fool head blown off!"

King ignored Lee's protests but began walking across the gangplank. "What is the meaning of this outrage? Where is Governor Narvez? I want an explanation immediately!" King insisted.

The general pulled his revolver out of his holster and fired a shot an inch from King's feet. King stopped dead in his tracks, his face pale and trembling. "Next time I aim for the *cojones,* señor. Perhaps that will have some effect on that loud mouth of yours. Make the voice a bit higher, maybe?" The general and the men within earshot laughed loudly and the joke spread quickly through the battalion. As quickly as he joked, the man turned serious again. "Get in line!" he shouted.

The general sent three of his men to inspect the ship to make sure there was no one left aboard except the captain. When the three had disappeared below deck, the general began to inspect the line. "You men are not soldiers," he said. "You are mere children. Does the United States Government send children to do a man's work?" Laughter rippled through the crowd again.

King could not control himself any longer. "Just what do you intend to do here?" he asked.

The general's anger flared. His temper seemed as unpredictable as a volcano. He placed the barrel of the gun against the bandage which still wrapped King's head. "I told you to be quiet. You will speak when you are spoken to. Is that understood?"

King nodded and looked to his right to see that his daughter was all right. The general noticed her too, and he immediately went to her side. "Well, well. Look what we have here. A blonde goddess from America." He ran his grimy fingers through her smooth, silky tresses. Then he took her chin between his thumb and forefinger and tilted her head from side to side. "Even better than a goddess," he murmured. "You're flesh and blood."

As he spoke, the three men he sent aboard the Rachel returned with the news that there was no one else aboard.

"Very good," the general said. "For *niños,* you follow your orders very well. Now," he said, turning to King once again. "Since you have the biggest mouth, and the biggest belly, you must be Señor King. Am I wrong?"

"I am King," said King, lowering his head.

"Just as I thought," said the general. "You see, I am quite perceptive. And you will soon see that I am not such a bad man as you think I am. Presidente Narvez would like to have a word with you before you begin your brave expedition."

"Presidente Narvez?" King asked, not understanding.

"Si. El Señor Narvez is presidente now."

King, still not quite understanding what the general meant, stepped out of the lineup and prepared to follow the general. If he had expected trouble, he had certainly not expected to be greeted in such a manner by the very people who invited them.

"The rest of you *niños* will remain in line," he heard the general saying, returning to his commanding tone. "The sun is very hot in Panama. You will soon get used to it." He broke off laughing again, and led King off into a nearby wood frame structure.

Lee had all but figured out what was going on. Narvez had taken control of the country and was intimidating the crew as a show of strength. What Narvez had planned for them, Lee did not know. Narvez could be owned by the railroad, but if that were the case, they would have been killed on the spot. Or he could be trying to play the railroads off against the U.S. Government, to gain some kind of advantage or support for his illegal government. Whatever the case, holding guns on a group of peaceful explorers was not the ideal gesture of friendship.

When the guards were not looking, O'Sullivan leaned over and nudged Lee in the side with his elbow.' "What do you think, Lee?" he said.

"The worst," replied Lee Morgan.

The inside of the building was dark and musty and reminded King very much of a barn. He wanted to ask the general more questions as he was led inside, but was afraid the volatile man might turn on him. For now, at least, he was being civil.

They entered a large room with three windows near the ceiling. The entire structure seemed to be about ready to collapse and King was reminded of the urban slums back in the States. Why did Narvez have me brought here? he thought to himself.

The general led him to a small table with two chairs on either side. He held one of the chairs for King and King seated himself. The general then left the room and King sat alone in the dim light for a few moments, alternately wondering what was going to become of his daughter and the rest of the crew, and trying to figure out why Narvez had gone to such extreme lengths to force this meeting with him. He had intended to meet with Narvez anyway. Why this show of force? And what did the general mean about Narvez being president? Panama was not an independent country. It was most surely under Colombian control!

The small-framed man entered the room and approached King. His dark hair was slicked back with grease and he carried a bottle and two glasses which he set in the middle of the table. He was dressed like a peasant and carried no weapon, unlike the soldiers outside. King decided to speak to him.

"When will I meet with Señor Narvez?" he asked.

The man looked at him oddly and sat across the table from King, filling the two glasses with rum from the labelless bottle. "I am Presidente Narvez," the man said. "Won't you join me in a gentleman's drink?"

King was taken aback. The man before him looked more like a day laborer than a politician. King was at a loss. How did he speak to this man?

"Why are you holding my crew and myself hostage?" he asked. "And since when have you called yourself president?"

"I have been president here since the great revolution two weeks ago. Panama is no longer under the jurisdiction of Colombia." The man took a sip from his glass and leaned forward in his chair. "Your men are not being held hostage. They are simply being detained for the moment. All of you will be free to go within the hour. My apologies if you were frightened. My troops are new recruits and I'm afraid General Cienfuegos is sometimes a bit . . . overzealous."

"I was not informed about a revolution, sir. I was not expecting to deal with you as president. But it doesn't matter. As you know, the U.S. Government is anxious to begin surveying in anticipation of a future canal. Am I to assume from the men outside that you are no longer willing to negotiate with my government?"

"Please do not assume that, Mr. King. On the contrary, I am most willing to talk whatever terms they wish. I apologize for my men. They are just my way of demonstrating that I do have control over the people of this country. And as their new leader, I want what is best for them. I am sure you can understand that. Just as your government wants what is best for your people."

"My government wants a canal built to transport ships and people from the Atlantic to the Pacific and back. They are considering several sites. Your . . . country is but one of them."

"Yes, but it is the most logical choice. This country is a mere fifty miles across and much of it is lake. In addition, the French have already got the project under way. Unfortunately, they had to cancel the project. It would be most wise for your government to resume the canal where they left off."

"What's your interest in the canal?" King asked.

"The more of your people that pass through Panama, the more prosperous my people will become. The railroad pays a handsome amount for the lease of the land we have given them. They have backed me in this revolution. I was given guns and military assistance. In return the railroads pay less money for the lands. That is why they support me. In return, my people do not have to share the wealth with Colombia."

"Sounds like a tidy little arrangement. So why your interest in the canal?" King asked.

"Look around you, Mr. King. Do you see opulence? I brought you here for a purpose. To see how my countrymen live. There is much hunger. In the cities there are slums which would shock you. Bandits pillage the villages. And without money I am powerless to do anything about it. The money I see from the railroads is nothing. And it would be a simple task for them to stop paying altogether. They can afford to hire Indians and drifters to do their fighting for them. My men are not strong enough to stop them.

"I need assistance from your government. Money. Food. Clothing. Arms for my soldiers. And most of all, independence. I will not bow to Colombia, the railroads, or your government. This land belongs to the people, not foreigners. We are willing to accept your presence, but you will not run this country."

"Are you saying we are free to go?"

"Of course. As I told you, I am most interested in seeing your government here—but on my terms. You will have safe passage and protection from my soldiers on the condition that you give me your word as a man of honor that you will deliver my message to your government."

"You have my word, Narvez." King could not bring himself to address the man as president. "I suspect that the railroad already knows we're here," King said. "And there's likely to be trouble with them. Won't it anger them even more if they know you are in league with us?"

"Please understand that I am not in league with you, Mr. King. I am simply looking out for my own interests. The same as you would do if you were in my position. My men will follow you from a distance. They will be dressed as Indians. The railroad will not suspect."

"Then I will return to my crew immediately. We will unpack here and leave in the morning as scheduled. I am sure the captain is anxious to return to familiar territory."

"The captain will not be returning," Narvez said bluntly. King stared worriedly at the man. He had not expected this new twist.

"What do you mean?" King asked cautiously.

"Exactly as I said," Narvez replied. "The vessel

will remain here with us. The captain is free to travel with you. But the ship will be detained."

"But why?"

"I am keeping it as a gesture of your good faith. So you will be sure not to forget the message I send. The captain is welcome to return for it once you have done so. Surely you did not think that your passage would be free. There is a price on everything, Mr. King."

"It would seem I have no choice. Will our weapons be returned?" King asked.

"You are quite correct, Mr. King. You may take anything you wish from the ship, including your arms. Even with them, you are outnumbered here, and without us you would not make it to the coast. However, the vessel will remain in our custody. Now, Mr. King, won't you stay and have another drink with me? Panamanian rum is quite a delicacy."

"Thank you, but I'm not exactly in a drinking mood at the moment. I should get back and tell the crew the news," King said.

"I'm sorry you feel that way, Mr. King. But I assure you, everything will work out for the best for all concerned. If, as you say, the railroad knows you are here, they will stop at nothing to prevent you from reaching Bilbao. How can you refuse my offer?"

King reluctantly admitted defeat. "As you said, I cannot."

"As a gesture of my good faith, I am providing you with a guide. Please excuse me a moment." Narvez rose and returned to the room from which he had entered. He was gone a few minutes and when he returned, he was leading a young Indian woman by the hand. King stood and nodded and the girl responded with a giggle.

"Please excuse her, Mr. King," Narvez said. "She does not mean to laugh at you. It is just that she is not used to American customs. In this country, Indian women are held in esteem among their people, but they are not treated with courtesy as you know it. Here, she is subservient in all respects." Narvez and King seated themselves again. The girl remained standing, waiting for orders.

"This is Maria," Narvez said. "She knows this country as well as any man alive. She will be your guide throughout your trip. You will find her an invaluable source of information and with her help you should have a speedy and safe journey through even the most treacherous of terrain."

King eyed the girl closely. "She is just a girl," he said.

"Do not let looks deceive you, Señor King," Narez said. "Maria is young and pretty, but she is a good scout and tracker. And she knows how to handle a gun. She proved herself quite valuable to the French."

"Then as much as I dislike this situation, I accept your offer, Narvez," King said.

"Good. Then you may return to your vessel and unpack your toys. I will instruct my men to assist you. I will leave it to you to break the news about the vessel to your captain."

King and his men spent the rest of the day unpacking and readying the gear. Crates containing the surveying equipment were opened and inspected for damage. Despite the water from the storm, everything seemed remarkably preserved.

Lee was just glad to be able to get his guns and whip back. King had charged him with overseeing the move from the ship to the building where King and Narvez had met. King had not counted on such inhospitable accommodations, but there was nowhere else to stay. At least Narvez had not *offered* anything else. Maybe he just wanted to give King a better idea of a peasant life in Panama.

King had asked Lee to inform the captain that the ship would have to stay. It was a job Lee had not wanted but he had relented when King explained that Johnson might try something foolhardy, and that Lee might be the better man to keep him calm.

Johnson was outraged, and threatened to pull out in the middle of the night, leaving behind everyone to fend for themselves. Lee convinced him that even if he did manage to get out to sea without being blown to bits under cannon fire, Johnson would never make it back to the States without a crew.

Ultimately, Johnson gave in, but not before swearing to get his revenge. The rest of the day he did no work, but sat glumly on the bridge with his head in his hands, wondering what was going to happen next.

As King had promised, Lee Morgan got to hand-pick the men for his small unit of guards. He chose only those who had been in the military at one time. They would be less likely to disobey orders. He also chose O'Sullivan, who had reservations about carrying around a lot of heavy weapons. All he wanted to do was photograph. He got a good start by choosing Narvez's men as his first subjects. They were more than willing to comply, each man more anxious than the previous to have his picture made with O'Sullivan's strange machine. Only Maria refused. The general said she thought it provoked evil spirits.

The final man Lee chose for his team was Captain Johnson. Lee picked him more out of sympathy than for his abilities. But the gesture seemed to bring the man out of his reverie. By evening he was looking forward to the new adventure.

Maria, King had discovered, spoke no English, and little Spanish. She had to rely on gestures to communicate. Lee had taken an immediate liking to her. He got through any message he wished using gestures alone. Maria understood, and understood that she had an admirer.

And she was something to admire, not only for her skills, but for her beauty and innocent mannerisms. Her long black hair was tied into a tight bun at the back of her head. Her eyes were like black pearls and pierced deeper than any knife. There was nothing false about her. If she didn't like you, it showed immediately. She simply ignored you. She didn't have to speak. King she didn't like. Lee she did. Lee saw her as the earthy woman Clarissa King could never be. Although Clarissa was definitely appealing, Maria was more so. Once she had met Lee Morgan, she never left his side.

The boat was unloaded by sundown and the captain went aboard to give it a final inspection. When he reached the bridge, he was tempted to start the engines and make a run for it, but with the ship tied instead of anchored, he knew that would be impossible.

Rather than stay in the musty building Narvez had provided, the crew decided to spend the final night before the journey aboard the ship. At least there they would not have to fend off the mosquitos for another night. King assigned Lee to stand watch over the supplies that had been stored indoors. Lee didn't find the prospect of staying awake all night slapping mosquitos pleasurable but he relented and the rest of the crew retired to the ship. O'Sullivan fashioned a small torch that would keep Lee's room lit for a few hours, but he would have to rely on candles for the rest of the night. He was glad that the moon was full, allowing some light to enter through the windows placed in the high ceiling of the room. As he bedded down on the wood and canvas cot he was given, he wondered what had happened to Maria. He had not seen her since the sun had gone down and he knew for certain she would not be allowed aboard the ship. Narvez's men were sleeping out in the open except for the handful assigned to guard duty.

Lee was just about to nod off when he heard a noise outside the window. It was a low moan that he, at first, thought must have been a wild animal that had scented their food stores. He ignored it, knowing that, whatever it was, there was no way that it could get inside. But then the noise came again, louder this time, and it was definitely human.

He rose, drawing one of the Colts from the gunbelt lying on the floor beside him and clasping his whip with the other hand. As he neared the door below one of the windows, he listened carefully, straining to make out the sound. There was a little gasp. Lee recognized Maria's voice. Thinking that she was being abused by one of Narvez's men, Lee quickly opened the door, his Colt aimed, ready to confront the man.

There was no one there but Maria. She was lying on the earth beside the building with blankets drawn up around her. She gasped as Lee stepped outside, and drew the blankets tightly around her. She looked terrified. Lee surveyed the scene, trying to detect anyone running or hiding nearby. There was no one.

Lee saw that the woman was naked beneath the blankets. Her face was drenched with sweat. As frightened as she looked, she seemed to be pleading with Lee, as if to ask him to help her. When he saw there had been no one with her, Lee realized what the woman had been doing, and why she had been sleeping right outside the door.

Lee smiled at the woman and nodded his head to indicate that she should come inside. The girl hesitated, then her pearly teeth broke through her dark perspiring face. She was embarrassed, but Lee Morgan had understood what she wanted. Yes, Lee Morgan had understood!

The girl got to her feet, still clutching the blankets around her body. She walked past Lee into the room, more excited now than frightened, though the dim torchlight inside made her afraid. Perhaps she should have stayed in the jungle with the rest of the soldiers. But they were so rough with her. She knew that they were only interested in pleasing themselves. Lee Morgan was different. Lee Morgan was an American and would be gentle.

Lee led her to the cot where he had been trying to

sleep. He sat on the edge and looked up at her. Their eyes met in the dim light and they held the contact for several minutes.

He knew the woman was not what he would have looked for back home. In Idaho, Indian women were treated no better than dirt, but even the most passionate Indian-hater found them sexually irresistible. Lee Morgan, though he admired the Indian way of life back home, was an exception. He wanted to talk to her, to tell her how beautiful she was, but there could be no words between them. There was only the night.

Maria broke away from his stare and looked down at the blankets covering her. She suddenly let them drop, revealing her taut young body to Lee. Lee leaned back and admired her figure: the slim waist and full womanly hips. Her breasts were browned and her nipples jutted out before her, turning hard as her skin met the cool night air. Her legs were muscular and smooth from hard labor and her lips were thick and pouty in anticipation.

"Lee Morgan—beautiful," she said.

Lee smiled at her attempt to speak his language, but said nothing in return. Instead he removed his shirt and boots and lay back on the cot, his eyes never leaving her nude form.

Maria sat next to him and Lee became even more aroused by the musky aroma of her sex as she moved nearer. Lee could not believe his good fortune. A woman so exotic he had not seen in all his life. Though she had labored all her life in the jungles where thousands had suffered, she still managed to maintain an innocent sensuality about her, something Lee Morgan was most grateful for at the moment. Her nude form stretched over him, her lips finding his, her tongue exploring his mouth with a ravenous passion.

She pulled away from him and struggled with his belt, tugging at it as though she had been waiting all her life for what she would find inside. Lee removed her hands and undid the belt, then slowly unbuttoned the trousers, delaying with each button as if to tease her and make her want him all the more. Even before he unfastened the last button, she was running her fingers tenderly through his hair, eagerly awaiting the chance to stroke his organ.

She pulled the trousers from his waist, past his knees and over his ankles, then turned to stare at him once again. Both of their naked bodies burned with anticipation as she ran her eyes over his lean frame to rest on his rapidly rising cock. She took it in her fingers and gently tugged the loose skin back and forth, each stroke making his organ taller and harder. She bent down and took the head in her mouth, stroking him even faster. She sucked to bring the blood up faster and rolled her tongue around him. When at last she stopped, she paused to look at her accomplishment. Lee's cock stood at full erection, jutting into the air and throbbing for more.

No words were spoken between them. Each knew what the other desired. Lee sat up and pointed to her crotch, indicating that he wanted to do for her what she had so easily done for him. Grasping her by the shoulders and laying her back onto the cot, Lee began to move over her body, kissing every inch. He nibbled her ears and her neck, then ran his tongue around her pert brown nipples. Then he traced a path down her stomach and took her thighs firmly in his calloused hands. He spread them easily, she only too eager to allow entry into her warmth.

Lee began by licking the inside of her thighs, enjoying every second of the heady smell surrounding her loins. Maria spread her legs apart even farther, allowing Lee easy entry into her wet pussy. Lee buried his face in the dark bush and opened his mouth over her slippery opening. His tongue darted out to meet her engorged clit and Maria gasped in pleasure as it slid over the tiny knob.

Lee gave her what she wanted, his tongue probing deep inside her, lapping at the juices which were now flowing freely. Maria shuddered and brought her legs together on each side of his head, clasping them around his back.

"Oh, Lee! Oh, Lee!" she cried, and then began moaning and speaking in a language Lee did not understand. But he did understand that he was giving this woman pleasure, a pleasure which she had evidently not known for some time, judging from the state of excitement she had been in when Lee caught her masturbating. She had wanted him, this rugged white man who had been so kind to her. And now she had him. Lee began moaning as well, which only served to increase the excitement. Her hips pumped so furiously that Lee thought she would swallow him whole if she could. She had his head in a vise grip between her legs. Lee let go of her thighs and slid his hands up her body to her breasts. He massaged their roundness and pinched the nipples gently, making them even harder than before.

Maria reached down and pushed his head even deeper into her. Lee knew she was about to come. He licked faster and, after pounding her clit with his tongue, plunged it deep into her. Maria let go of his head and gripped the sides of the cot.

"Ooooohhh," she moaned, then bucked one last time and lay still. She still held Lee's head tightly between her legs, not letting him move away from her until she had savored every last second of his presence there. When finally she let go, Lee's face was drenched with her juices.

Her orgasm had been intense, but Maria wanted more. She pulled Lee on top of her, forcing him to put all of his weight over her body. Between her legs, Lee's cock probed to find her opening. Maria grabbed the rod and led it to the entrance of her slit, pausing to rub it gently across her clit. They both gasped at the pleasure of it, her expression showing Lee that he was everything she wanted.

Lee marveled at the way this innocent woman knew his every desire. She was not slow to respond. Lee had not known many women who responded with such eagerness and abandon.

Lee pulled away until his cock almost left her body, but she pulled him back to refill her drenched hole. He took the initiative, pumping her furiously until both of their bodies were wracked with exertion and bathed in sweat.

On the brink of letting his load explode into her, Lee slowed and stopped his pounding thrusts, letting his cock remain still inside her, letting her feel the pulsing rod swell even larger. Finally, he couldn't stand it any longer and began thrusting with even more vigor.

Maria was in ecstasy. Wave after wave of orgasm shook her body, sending chills through her and flushing her face. When she was entirely spent, she pushed Lee to his knees and forced him to come out. Lee wondered what she was up to. As he sat on his knees, his throbbing member straining before him, stretching out over her body, Maria again took him in her hands. Such a beautiful cock Maria had never seen. She stared at it and stroked it with such curiosity that Lee thought it might have been her first. His cock stood at an angle pointing toward the ceiling, purpling and ready to burst. Then he understood. Maria wanted to watch him come. Lee slid closer to her, so that his cock stretched over her stomach. Maria picked up the pace, pulling his foreskin back and forth, watching it cover the swelling head as she pulled it outward.

Lee was ready. He pumped his hips as she held her hands in position, letting them act as an even tighter cunt. Lee leaned back, his hands on her knees, thrusting his cock toward her to give her the best view.

He gave a tremendous shudder and then it came, spurt after spurt of hot semen shooting from his slit, into the air and onto her body. She kept pumping him, urging every drop of the sticky milk from his balls. Lee was stunned. Never had he come so violently and so much. And still it did not stop shooting. Maria's belly was covered and her breasts were splattered with his load.

She held Lee tightly as he recovered, and with her free hand she ran her fingers through the liquid, spreading it over her and letting the air dry it.

When Lee finally regained his senses, he lay

beside her again, covering her face and neck with tender, grateful kisses. They both lay still and spent, unable to speak to one another and not needing to even if they could. They both knew that the morning would bring hard work and new priorities. But for now they had each other, though both knew well that their night of pleasure might never be repeated. As Lee lay on his back, beginning to drift off to sleep, he thought of the many other women he had known. While many, including his wife, had given him much pleasure, none had excited him with the same exotic passion he had found with this poor Indian girl.

Lee looked over at her who had given him so much. She ran her fingers over his face and through the thick hair on his chest.

"Lee Morgan—beautiful," she said. And Lee was thinking the same about her.

He awoke later that night not knowing where he was in the dark. Something was happening to him; he felt strangely excited again. Then he realized that Maria was between his legs with his limp organ in her mouth, trying to raise it again. Lee felt the surge in his loins and they made love again.

When the cook rang the bell for breakfast, Maria was gone.

7

Morning arrived as sticky and humid as the day before. At breakfast, the crew seemed to be divided between those dreading the long overland trip and those anxious about the possibility of their protectors turning on them. After all, they had already confiscated their ship. Who knew what else they might do?

Lee Morgan was in no mood for small talk at breakfast. When he awoke, Maria was nowhere to be found. He understood that she had left so as not to be caught in bed with Lee in the morning, but he had not seen her since rising and her disappearance concerned him. Maybe she was just too embarrassed to face him.

Tim O'Sullivan noted Lee's sullen appearance but thought it was just because he had stayed awake all night guarding the supplies. Until breakfast, O'Sullivan had hardly paid him any mind. He had been too busy with his cameras and meters to think of much else, least of all the danger that might be awaiting them in the jungle.

Lee had had three cups of Cook's dishwater coffee but had hardly touched his food when O'Sullivan sat on the ground next to him.

"Scorcher, ain't it?" he said cheerfully, trying to draw Lee out.

"Might as well get used to it," Lee said.

"Mighty fine mood you're in today. Something eating at you, Lee?"

Lee tried to cover up his concern over what had happened to Maria. "Naw, just getting nervous about this trip. I got a funny feeling this ain't going to go as smoothly as King thinks."

"Don't let it get to you," O'Sullivan said. "We can handle ourselves. You got the men you wanted and from what I can see, they're already scared enough to shoot first and ask questions later. 'Sides, we got all them soldier boys to back us up. They'll be right behind us every step of the way."

"That's just what worries me. Those fellows are likely to start shooting us if we're attacked."

"You may be right, but I'm inclined to trust them for now. Narvez seems like an honorable man. Remember, we haven't got much choice anyway."

Lee downed the rest of the coffee and tossed what was left of his meal over his shoulder into the tall grass behind him. There was suddenly a rustling behind him as if the action had disturbed something. Lee looked cautiously around the tree he was leaning against. Not ten feet in back of him was the biggest snake he had ever seen, poised and ready to strike. It could not have reached the two men where they sat, but O'Sullivan jumped to his feet and backed off several paces.

Lee ducked back behind the tree and slowly pulled out his Colt. Then he swung back around and snapped off a shot. The snake's head exploded into hundreds of bits of flesh, then it lay limp on the ground.

Lee stood up and dusted off the seat of his pants and reholstered his gun. O'Sullivan stared at him, amazed that Lee could hit a target as small as a snake's head without so much as taking time to aim.

"Never trust a snake in the grass," Lee said and walked off to get another cup of coffee.

Maria finally returned to camp. When Lee caught up with her, she smiled sheepishly at him and looked at her feet. When Lee looked concerned, she made gestures demonstrating that she had been washing, and Lee understood that she had gone upstream some distance to bathe privately. Lee couldn't believe a woman so modest could make love the way she had the night before.

The expedition got under way without a hitch. Everyone was anxious to get going, Lee being no exception. Despite his reservations, he wanted to get the whole thing over and done with as soon as possible. He suddenly felt a desire to be back on his ranch, riding one of his best stallions into town to pay a call on Suzanne Clemmons.

The first day out, King and his men set up camp near the French canal site, to examine the progress that had been made. They hadn't even made the cut through to Lake Gatun. King was in his glory now; he had everything under control. His differences with Lee were the furthest things from his mind as he set up the surveying equipment and recorded the precise measurements in his notebooks. He took note of the types of plant life, the height of trees, the depth and height of valleys and rises. Soil samples were taken and information on the weather was recorded. The men King had hired were professionals in their field. And despite their lack of skill on the ship and in other aspects of the expedition, Lee had to admire the speed and efficiency with which they worked under King's orders.

Lee was by no means idle. When he was not helping O'Sullivan set up his camera equipment, and fending off the huge swarms of mosquitos that seemed to descend upon the party and then disappear without pattern, he was scouting out the trail with Maria and organizing teams of men with machetes to cut through the dense jungle underbrush where there were no trails. Under the tropical sun, vegetation grew so fast that if a path were not used frequently, the jungle would reclaim it.

Lee and Maria had gone far ahead of the main group when they saw their first Indian. He had been hiding some twenty yards ahead of them under cover of the thick brush. It was Maria who had spotted him. Lee was amazed at her sharp eyes. The vegetation had been so thick that Lee might have walked right past the man without ever having seen him. When Maria pointed to him, he simply turned and walked out of sight, not caring whether he had been seen or not.

Lee understood this not to be a threat, but rather a warning to the whole group that they were being watched. When they returned to camp, Lee reported the sighting to King.

"How many were there?" he blustered. The man was visibly alarmed.

"Only one," Lee said. "Didn't seem to be looking for a fight. Just turned and walked away when we spotted him."

"Trouble or not, I'm not taking any chances. Are you sure it wasn't one of Narvez's men? They're supposed to be keeping an eye on us."

"Looked pretty damn real to me! Besides, Narvez's men wouldn't be wandering out in that jungle alone."

"Well, there may be others. But I doubt if they're going to attack us. We couldn't possibly have anything they could want."

"Unless he's a scout for someone else," Lee alluded.

"Like I said," King repeated, "I'll take no chances. Round up your men and have them posted all around this area. Have them report anything suspicious."

Lee sent his men out in pairs to wander the outskirts of the base and King went back as if he were on another world. Everything fascinated him and he took more plant and insect specimens on that first day than he knew he could ever carry back to the States.

By the time the camp was set up for the night, the whole party was exhausted from the combination of hard labor and the stifling humidity. Sleep was more on their minds than Cook's paltry supper.

By nightfall there were several fires going in the hopes that the smoke would keep the monstrous onslaught of mosquitos away for the evening.

Lee and O'Sullivan were sitting in the light of one of the fires eating their supper of potatoes and beans, and O'Sullivan was boring Lee with all the details of the day's shooting.

"Got some great shots of the French canal," he was saying. "It is simply amazing that they could even consider shipping supplies and men all the way across the Atlantic for a folly like that. Hell, it'd be a miracle if we ever get it finished, and we're practically around the corner. It's no wonder they gave up on it."

Lee took another bite of beans and looked up at the man who was showing renewed enthusiasm for the project. "The wonder is that we were fool enough to get talked into this madness."

As he spoke, King walked up with his plate and cup. "I heard that, Morgan. And I'll ask you to refrain from such talk. My boys are tired and hungry. You don't have to put the fear of God into them as well."

Lee glared at the man and took another bite of beans, using his spoon to wipe the juice from his chin. King spread out a little blanket and plunked his fat body down next to O'Sullivan, making sure to put some distance between him and the volatile Morgan. "All our men report back?" he asked. "Any new sightings?"

Lee took a sip of the bottled water Cook had brought along for drinking. Even he had heard the stories about what happened to those who drank from the native supplies. "No one saw anything," he said. "But then I wouldn't have seen the one I did if it hadn't been for Maria. They're pretty good at keeping out of sight when they want to."

"Everyone report back?" King asked.

"Yeah," Lee said. "But I sent two back to scout out where we saw the first one about an hour ago. Shoulda been back by now, come to think of it."

"You sent two men out there this close to dark!" King exclaimed. "What the hell do you think you're doing, Morgan?"

"Following your orders. You wanted lookouts. You got 'em. But we're going to have to take a few chances. There just ain't enough of us to go sending a dozen men out every time we hear a noise. Those boys will be back soon. The trail's clear for about a mile, and they can find their way back, no problem. And they both know how to use a gun."

"But . . ."

"Look," Lee said, becoming irritated. "If you don't like it, you're welcome to go out looking for them yourself. But I'm going to give them another half hour. If they're not back, I'll go out hunting for them myself. What time you have, Tim?"

Tim looked at his watch and shrugged his shoulders. The damn thing had stopped. "Maybe the humidity; probably rusted it out. Who the hell needs the time out here, anyway?"

When the men did not return, Lee himself began to worry. It might have been foolish to send two men out alone that late in the day, but Lee was not going to admit it, not even to himself.

He quietly gathered up a party of four, and made sure they were well armed with rifles and machetes. Maria indicated that she wanted to go along and Lee was in no position to turn her down. In the dark, with little light filtering through the jungle growth, he was going to need everyone he could get, especially one who knew the terrain.

The group marched along the narrow trail single file, the walls of jungle threatening to close in on them. If a man were to step more than a few yards off the trail, he might very well be lost forever.

Lee led the group, with Maria right on his heels. They paused every few steps to allow Maria to listen and the men to get their bearings. It was slow going and Lee hoped they wouldn't have to be gone too long. If the camp were to come under attack, the men Lee had left behind would not be able to hold the fort for long, especially with King in charge. And who knew when Narvez's men might arrive—if at all. In fact, Lee thought, they might be the very ones to do the attacking.

They had gone no more than 500 yards when Maria stopped dead in her tracks. She stared straight ahead for a moment and then came up behind Lee, pointing over his shoulder. Lee saw nothing, but indicated that the men behind him were to drop down. Lee and Maria took a few steps farther ahead and then Lee saw them. Two bodies lying on the edge of the path, barely visible. Through his shock, Lee wondered again at this woman's keen sense of sight. Though Lee's tracking skills were nothing to sneeze at back home, he might have stumbled over the two bodies if Maria hadn't pointed them out. Waving the other men to follow, Lee cautiously approached the bodies and discovered that they were indeed the two men he had sent out.

But what, or who, had gotten to them? It was as if both men dropped where they stood. There was no indication of a struggle and neither man had drawn a weapon. There was no a drop of blood to be seen.

Now Lee was frightened. How was it that these seasoned men could have been killed so easily, so silently, and so near the camp? And the most mysterious question of all—why were they killed in the first place? Narvez had said there were no Indian villages nearby, and there should be no problem until they reached the other side of the lake.

Lee bent and hoisted one of the men over his shoulder. "Taylor," Lee whispered to the biggest man in the group. "Get up here and get this other man. We're going back to camp pronto. If these fellows are still alive, Doc may be able to save them." But the look in Maria's eyes told him they were not.

The burly guard easily lifted the man and the group began walking quickly and quietly back to camp. Lee brought up the rear, turning often to check the trail and jungle behind them.

"My God! What the hell happened out there?" King shouted when they returned. He had been sitting, drinking a cup of tea with his daughter and Newport around one of the open fires. Clarissa let out a gasp, but Newport looked on as staid as ever. Lee and Taylor lay the bodies on the ground side by side.

"Well, don't just stand there gawking," Lee shouted. "Somebody get the doc." One of the guards from the group that found the men ran to get the doctor while Lee pushed everyone back into a circle around the two bodies.

"You got me, King. I don't know what happened to them any more than you do. Just found 'em laying on the side of the trail and I don't think they're gonna be walking no more."

Lee bent to check the pulse of the man nearest him. He found none. As he stood, the doctor arrived and had to push men out of the way to get through the circle.

"Good Lord!" the doctor said when he saw the bodies. "What happened to them?"

"You tell me, Doc. We just found them out there. Don't think nothing human got them. They didn't even draw their guns. Like they weren't expecting nothing. If someone killed them, they didn't even bother to take what they had on them. Maybe a snake got 'em."

The doctor bent over the two men and checked their pulse and to see if they were still breathing. They weren't.

"Bring them into my tent," he ordered. "They're both dead, but I'll look them over and see if I can find what did them in." He stood and strode quickly away.

Lee pointed at Taylor and another man and they understood that they were to carry the bodies. Then he turned to King and Newport. King was still staring mutely, his jaw looking as if it would drag the ground if his mouth were any wider. Newport sipped his tea.

"Newport," Lee said quietly. "You seem awfully calm about all of this."

"Mr. Morgan, surely you did not expect to come into this harsh land without some loss of life. The government has sent me on expeditions such as this all over the globe—to places I'm sure you've never even heard of. This is quite usual to me and does not shock me in the least. On the contrary, I'm surprised something of this nature has not occurred before now. Be thankful, Mr. Morgan, that it is not you in their shoes." Newport tossed the rest of his cold tea on the ground and walked away. Lee stared after him, dumbfounded.

King, Lee, and Maria went directly to the doctor's tent and had to push their way past the men waiting for news of what had caused their comrades' death. The doctor had them stretched out on two cots, stripped to their shorts, and was examining one of the unfortunate men's chest. "Come here," he said, "and look at this. I've never seen anything quite like it." Lee and King came closer while Maria stood in the shadows near the flap of the tent. As they bent down, the doctor pointed to a small puncture wound in the man's chest. "I don't know what killed them, but seeing there ain't another mark on them, I figger this must be it." He held aloft a small dart no bigger than a large fly. "Found one of these stuck in each of them. Looks like a dart of some sort."

Maria's eyes widened at the sight of the dark. She had seen many men struck down by these. The poison the jungle Indians tipped them with could paralyze a man in seconds, kill him within minutes.

Lee saw the horror in Maria's eyes as the doctor spoke. Lee picked up one of the darts carefully so as not to touch the tip and held it before him as he approached Maria.

"You know what this is, Maria?" Lee said sternly. And then more gently, "Tell us if you do. It's very important."

The woman understood his meaning but not his words, and Lee could clearly see that she was frightened.

"Tell us!" he repeated.

Maria slowly raised her hand to her mouth and made an open fist. Then she blew hard through the opening in her hand and ran from the tent in terror.

"Blowgun!" King said, his face almost as contorted as Maria's had been. "She was trying to tell us that these men were killed with a blowgun. No wonder there was no struggle. The bastards killed them before they even knew they were being attacked."

"That would seem to be about the size of it," the doctor said. "We'd better get these fellows buried fast. Infection spreads quickly in these parts. No need to leave them lying around for the mosquitos to eat up."

The doctor stepped out of the tent to round up some of the dead men's friends to help bury them. As soon as he had left, Lee turned to King. "What do you know about blowguns? I've never heard of such a thing."

King looked surprised at Lee's ignorance. "A blowgun is a thin, hollow tube that the natives use to shoot darts. The darts are prepared with poisons they concoct from the plants down here. Don't ask me which ones. They use them in warfare in lieu of guns. As you can see, they kill quickly and efficiently, and best of all, they don't make any noise. If you want more information, check with Newport. He's the expert."

Lee looked at the man oddly. "How does Newport come to be such an expert? And what do you know about that man, anyway? He's starting to sound mighty suspicious to me. Did you see how he acted when we brought these fellows back? It was like he expected us to find them dead."

"Now, Morgan, don't get all hotheaded and jump the gun. Newport is an agent of the United States Government. Like he said out there, he's had experience in many matters of this sort. He's been on a dozen expeditions all over the world and was an adventurer long before he came to work for Washington."

"Adventurer? Mercenary is more like it. He ever been down here before?"

"Not to Panama, exactly. He was sent to Nicaragua a couple of years back with a handful of men to scout out another river passage to Lake Nicaragua. They were checking on a route up the Indio River. They should have sent a larger party. The bastard was lucky to get out alive. The entire party was killed and Newport managed to get out on a homemade raft. Indians got them." King reflected on this a minute and suddenly saw what Lee was getting at. The expedition was starting out exactly as had Newport's previous venture into Central America.

"Lee, I hate to admit that you may be right about him, but I still don't think we should jump to any conclusions. We don't convict a man on circumstantial evidence back home."

"This ain't back home," Lee said. "And if you ain't got no objections, I'm having him watched twenty-four hours a day from here on in. If he's up to something, we'll soon find out."

"All right. You may be right. Just don't alarm any of the others, and make sure the men you choose to watch don't let on to the others what they're up to. No need to cause a panic. We're not going to hang a man on suspicion."

"That sits just fine with me," Lee said. "But if it turns out he is up to something, I've got first crack at him. I ain't had a good feeling about him since I first laid eyes on him."

King and Lee left the tent just as the doctor was coming in to tend to the bodies again. As they walked back to the fire where O'Sullivan, Newport, and Clarissa were now sitting, they stopped for a moment to watch several men with picks and shovels digging two shallow graves in the clearing.

No one spoke as Lee and King joined the group. All had seen the men digging the graves and thus knew the men were dead.

"What's to become of us?" Clarissa said wistfully.

"Hell if I know," Lee said, looking sideways at Newport, who had poured a fresh cup of tea. "We'd best keep our eyes and ears open right now. We'll keep on schedule and start across Gatun by tomorrow morning. By that time King ought to have his surveying done on this side of the lake."

"I agree," said King. "There's nothing we can do at the moment. We will simply let come what may and hope for the best. I just hope Narvez is a man of his word."

Everyone slept uneasily that night. Aside from the other camp guards, Lee posted John Taylor to keep a close eye on Newport's tent. Lee half hoped that Maria would visit his tent again in the night, but as soon as his head hit the cot, he thought better of the idea. He needed the rest. And so, probably, did she. They'd both had a rough day and Maria was most likely still in tears over the discovery of the darts.

Lee wondered what Clarissa was thinking. She must be scared out of her wits. She was a strong-willed woman, but the fact that her father did not even warn her about the possibility of danger did not sit easy with Lee Morgan. He hated himself for not informing her of the possibilities when he had the chance.

After his fitful night's sleep, Lee rose early and went directly to Cook's tent. He woke the man out of a sound sleep, kicking the boots Cook had not bothered to remove before retiring. "Wake up, you old dog," Lee whispered loudly. "I've got a couple of questions for you."

"W-what?" Cook muttered, still half asleep. "Who is it? What do you want?"

Then he drifted off again.

Lee kicked him again and the old man sat straight up. He brushed the stringy gray hair away from his face and rubbed his eyes to see who would wake him while it was still dark. "Oh, it's you."

"Yeah, it's me. And I've got a couple of questions I want answered, so get up." The man stared at Lee as if he were out of his mind.

"What kind of questions?" Cook asked, wondering whether Morgan had found his stash of booze.

"Remember that fire at the pier?" Lee asked.

"Remember it? How could I forget it? That'll be some story to tell in my old age, heh, heh. Damn near got killed."

"You didn't get a scratch on you. Now, I want you

to tell me everything you can remember about it."

"I told you all I know the night it happened. I'd been drinking a little, you know, so things are a little fuzzy. I can't rightly remember as much as I should."

"Humor me. Let's go over it one more time. You were out on the dock, right?"

"Yeah. I was just finishin' off a pint I'd found in one of the lifeboats when I seen this fellow kinda snooping around across the way, like he was lookin' for something, you know. As soon as he saw me lookin' at him, he walked away like he was in a hurry to get someplace."

"Or in a hurry to get away," Lee said. "Do you remember anything about what this fellow looked like? Could you see his face?"

"Naw, it was almost dark. I couldn'ta made him out even if I was sober. He was a tall guy, over six foot, I'd say. Was wearing a black suit, or almost black. Hard to tell in the light."

"Was he carrying anything that you noticed?"

"Why, yeah, come to think of it, he was. He had a little black box or something under his arm, looked like a present 'cept for the color. Hey, I'd almost forgotten about that."

Some present, Lee thought. "That's good. Do you remember anything else?"

Cook yawned and lay back on the ground. "Naw, now let me sleep. What do you want to know all that for? Ain't nothin' you can do about it now. Fellow got clean away."

"Maybe there is something I can do about it. Do you remember that Detective Pinker that kept hanging around?"

"You think he did it? Lord, Lee, the man was a policeman. He wouldn't try to blow up a boat. 'Sides, it warn't him. I'd have known him a mile away. Got to admit that that feller did look a mite familiar. Can't place him, though, if that's what you're after."

"Well, thanks for your help, Cook." Lee started backing out of the man's tent and bumped his head on a pan hanging on one of the support posts.

"Cain't say I been none," Cook said. "Now get out of here and let me sleep. And don't you wake me till dawn."

Lee left the tent and turned back to close the flap. The man's boots were sticking out the end and Lee gave them a kick. "Why're you sleeping with your boots on, Cook?" Lee whispered.

"Keeps the skeeters off," came the reply.

Back in his tent, Lee thought over what Cook had told him. He still could not prove anything, but his suspicion of Newport was mounting. The man who set off the explosion in New Orleans fit Newport's description, but so did about a thousand other men in the city. Lee had ruled out Pinker. Cook was right. Pinker had been anxious about what King was up to, but he would not risk going afoul of the law to find out what it was. Lee was just going to have to wait it out and hope that he was wrong about Newport.

After breakfast, Lee immediately went to where Taylor was packing for the long hike to the lake and asked about Newport. Taylor reported nothing unusual. Newport had not stirred during the night. Lee really didn't expect the man to be so obvious, but he would maintain the guard.

The trek to the lake was uneventful. Everyone carried what they could on their backs. Lee and a few other men carried light loads in case they had to spring into action quickly. Lee's guards were placed strategically throughout the party, rifles at the ready. As the men passed by the site of the previous night's murders, they were especially watchful. Another attack might come from the same area. King was relieved when nothing happened.

They reached the lake well before noon. A temporary camp was established, and while King and one group set up their surveying equipment and tested the depth of the water, Lee took another group and began building the rafts they would need to cross the placid lake.

Gatun was deceptive. On the surface it appeared to be a calm sheet of glass, reflecting the brilliant sunlight and the lush tropical jungle surrounding it. What wasn't immediately apparent were the huge crocodiles that infested the water, feeding on anything that was unlucky enough to fall in. Then there was the danger of an Indian attack. The Indians could easily attack them from the shore as the group paddled around the lake.

"Think those Indians will make their move?" O'Sullivan was asking Lee while on a break from his morning's shoot.

"Sure as hell hope not," Lee said. "They could take us mighty easy on the open water. And there ain't no place to run 'cept in the water."

Lee wasn't too worried about being caught on the water. If he was right about Newport, no attack would come while the man behind it all was in the way. Lee believed he was right when they paddled into the smooth green water in the early afternoon. The water did not look murky, but the dense plant life did not let him see the bottom, even in the shallowest of water. No one cared to guess what lay beneath.

Once they had shoved off, there was very little talking. The group of rafts slid quietly across the water. Everyone gawked at the brightly colored birds and the luminescent silver fish that came so close to the surface that they could almost be caught with bare hands.

Lee kept his eyes peeled for any sight of Indians, and his men were kept on constant guard. Though Newport did not seem to be up to anything suspicious, Lee noted that the man did stay very low on the raft.

"Seen anything?" O'Sullivan was asking. He had been using a hand-held camera rather than his usual tripod to photograph scenes of the Gatun shoreline not twenty yards away.

"Nothing but birds and bugs," Lee said. "I kinda been keepin' an eye out behind us, but there ain't been no sign of Narvez or his toy soldiers."

"You think he might have abandoned us?"

"Hell, I don't think they was ever following us in the first place. They just wanted our boat. What do they care what happens to us? They could take us themselves if they wanted to."

"Lee, you know they ain't gonna do that. If they'd wanted us dead, they would have seen to it back in Cristobal."

"Maybe they just want to torture us a little, see how bad those Indians can hurt us before they move in for the kill. Hey, give me that camera of yours a minute!''

O'Sullivan reluctantly turned it over to him. "Here, but be careful. That's an expensive piece of equipment. What do you want it for anyway? See a good shot?''

Lee grabbed the camera and turned in around several times looking for the viewfinder. "What are you talking about, Tim? This thing works like a telescope, don't it? Can't it make things far away seem close up?''

"Yeah," O'Sullivan said.

Lee could not believe the man did not see his meaning. "Well, then, get over here and show me how the damn thing works." With O'Sullivan's camera, Lee would have a commanding view of the entire area.

"You just look through the viewfinder there and point it in the direction you want to look. If you want a sharper picture, just turn that little knob on the side of the lens. That's all there is to it, unless, of course, you want to take a shot. Then you have to push that button on the top. That opens the shutter and takes the picture. Got all that?'' O'Sullivan smiled at Lee's sudden interest in photography. He'd never known Lee to be the cultural sort.

Lee first looked toward the horizon behind them. There was still no sign of anyone following them, either on rafts on on foot. Ahead there was nothing but more shore and the seemingly endless expanse of water. And in the jungle there was no trace that humans had ever been there.

"Not a damn thing happening out there," Lee said discouraged. He was just about to hand the camera

back to O'Sullivan when he swung it around and
scanned the other rafts in the area. On one, he saw
King arguing with one of his men over some sort of
instrument. Clarissa was sitting nearby brushing
her tangled hair and using the opportunity to rest to
preen instead. Shifting his gaze, he saw Maria hard
at work paddling one of the rafts, matching the
effort of the men aboard stroke for stroke.

On the same raft, Lee saw Newport. The man
seemed to be rummaging through one of his bags for
something lost.

"How about giving me the camera back now,
Lee," O'Sullivan insisted. He was becoming
concerned that Lee might drop it in the water where
there be no chance of getting it back.

"Just a minute," Lee said, stepping a bit closer to
the edge of the raft and turning the dial O'Sullivan
had mentioned to get a clearer picture.

Lee could see that Newport had found what he
had been looking for, and turned the dial to see the
image for himself. Lee's mouth fell open. The man
was examining the contents of a smallish black box.

Lee snapped the picture.

8

The next three days brought no incident to the expedition. The first night they had camped out on the shore of the lake, but there had been no sign of Indians. Even Maria seemed more relaxed. The next day the going was much rougher. It was then that they were forced to cross the largest body of water to the other side of the many-fingered lake. They strained to reach the shore before dark and all were exhausted by the time the sun set. There was still no sign of Narvez's men and no other rafts were seen on the horizon that day. The fourth day had brought them to the part of the lake where they would abandon their rafts and set out on foot once again.

Maria led the way, for there was not much of a trail, and King kept track of their progress with his maps and compass.

Boredom was setting in. Day after day of water and jungle took their toll on the party. Most were lethargic, not wanting to work. Even King's spirits had dampened somewhat. He seemed just to want to get the rest of the job done in a hurry and get back to the States where he could move on to some other project. Some of the men were exhibiting slight fevers, and some were suffering from diarrhea so bad they could not even work. The dampness and heat were taking their toll on O'Sullivan as well. He hacked and wheezed until Lee thought he was going to spit up his lungs. His camera equipment rarely saw the light of day now; he merely sat with his back against a tree while King went about his duty.

That fourth day Lee was as wary as ever. After seeing Newport sifting through the contents of his black box, exactly the same as Cook had described, he was certain the man had been behind the bombing in New Orleans.

"Taylor," Lee said to the guard he trusted most while they were setting up the fires in the evening. "You noticed anything suspicious about Newport since I asked you to keep an eye on him?"

"Not a thing, Morgan," Taylor said, shrugging his shoulders. "The man helps King all day and then goes to his tent right after dark. I don't see nothing of him again till morning. What you think he's up to?"

"I don't know yet and I can't prove a thing about him. But I sure as hell intend to, and when I do, I'll make sure he hangs. Now listen, there's one more thing I want you to do."

"What's that?"

"Newport's carrying with him a canvas bag that I guess he stores his gear in. In it there's a black box of some sort. It ain't locked. I know because I saw him checking into it a couple of days back. But he thinks I suspect something about him so he's watching me as close as I'm watching him. Now, look, he don't carry that bag with him everywhere he goes, so I want you to see if you can get a peek into it when he's off eating or asleep.''

"And what kind of explaining are you suggesting I do if he catches me at it? Tell him I accidentally walked into the wrong tent, opened the wrong bag, and looked in the wrong black box?''

"That's something you're going to have to figure out for yourself. But if you're careful, you won't get caught. You game?''

"Hell, I'll do it. But only because you asked and think it's important. I ain't gonna feel good about rummaging through a man's personal things.''

Lee could understand the man's feelings. But he was so sure about his suspicions that he decided to tell the man what he thought.

"Let me let you in on something that might make you feel a little better,'' Lee said as quietly as he could. "I got a feeling that Newport was the man who blew up the pier the night before we left. Cook said he saw a man hanging around that fit his description. And that man was carrying a black box just like Newport's got. And I want to see just what he's got in there. Not only that, but I've got a hunch he's got something much bigger up his sleeve, and I want you to help me find out what it is.''

By this time Taylor was almost bug-eyed. "You think he might have had something to do with those boys who was darted to death?'' he said.

"Not directly. He couldn't have gotten away from camp without someone noticing, and even if he could he wouldn't go wandering around in that jungle by himself. No, I think he's up to something much bigger. I just can't put my finger on it.''

"You think he's dangerous?"

"Well, he carries a gun on his side, but so does every other man. If you're asking me if he'd kill in cold blood, I can't give you an answer.''

After supper, Lee and O'Sullivan sat around one of the fires talking over old times, O'Sullivan telling stories about the mischief Lee had gotten into in his teen years. Both were drinking lukewarm tea, though O'Sullivan was feeling so bad that he would have given anything for a cup of warm milk at that moment.

There was some kind of activity on the other side of camp and Lee jumped up, cutting O'Sullivan off midsentence, to see what the matter was. Maria was pointing off into the depths of the jungle at something everyone was straining to see. Evidently, whoever it was had disappeared, but Maria was still terrified. As she saw Lee Morgan approach, she ran to his arms. He held her for a moment, then pushed her to an arm's length. He stared into her wet eyes as if to ask what was wrong. Through her crying she managed to make the same gesture she had used before to indicate the blowgun.

"Looks like we might have some company tonight,'' Lee said to the crowd that had gathered. "I'm going to have to enlist some of you other fellows as guards. We'll have a constant heavy watch from here on in. No use in any more of us getting killed without a fight. Taylor, I want you to round up all the available men you can find. They'll work shifts all night.''

The men dispersed and Lee led Maria over to where he and O'Sullivan had been sitting. "Maria thinks she saw someone else out there," King said to O'Sullivan.

"Another Indian? Anyone hurt?"

"No one was hurt. It was most likely one of those from the same group that had their eyes on us on the other side of the lake. Like Narvez said, this is the home stretch. Tomorrow, we'll be within a few hundred yards of the railroad. If we're going to be attacked in force, that will be the time. If we are and we make it through, we catch the boat waiting in the gulf the next afternoon."

"Damn good thing, too. I don't think I could take much more of this heat. Cough's getting worse every day, too."

It was well into the night when Taylor approached Newport's tent. Despite the mosquitos, Newport was one of the few to sleep with the flaps of his tent open. He claimed to have some kind of repellent to keep them away, but Lee thought it made him smell like a skunk in a cedar chest.

Taylor had come upon the tent quietly. If the man woke, his excuse would be that he heard a noise and thought that some wild animal was prowling nearby. He still didn't know what he was going to say if he was caught red-handed with Newport's bag. He couldn't very well blame Lee Morgan, especially since he was doing this on his own volition.

The bag Lee had mentioned was sitting just inside Newport's tent and Taylor managed to reach in and lift it without disturbing the snoring man. He knew he could not rummage through the man's belongings right there. The noise would wake him for sure. He stealthily slung the bag over his shoulder and, stepping lightly, carried it just outside the camp to the edge of the lake where he was supposed to be keeping guard.

With a small torch planted firmly in the ground, Taylor sat down to examine the contents of the bag. At first glance there seemed to be nothing there but clothes and personal items, but then Taylor saw what Lee was after. At the bottom there was the black box.

He had wondered why the bag was heavier than it looked and now he knew. He maneuvered the other contents and worked the box loose. It was not locked and the latch was easy to operate. Taylor wondered what could be so important to Lee Morgan. When he opened it, Taylor's eyes nearly popped out of his head. Inside, there were several neat rows of dynamite, enough to blow the whole camp back to New Orleans. There also seemed to be some kind of timing device, but Taylor did not know its significance. No wonder Lee was so concerned. It was evident that Newport could very well have blown a hole in the pier. Taylor carefully replaced the box in the bag and covered it over with clothes. If he was careful, Newport would never know it had been disturbed and Taylor could report back to Lee his startling discovery. Taylor got to his feet and hefted the bag to his shoulder once again.

"Well, good evening, Mr. Taylor. Beautiful night for a stroll, isn't it?" Taylor jerked around to comfront the voice and saw that Newport was standing in his path with a gun leveled at his chest. The guard had no chance to raise a weapon to the man. All he could do was stand there and hope that Newport did not plan to kill him. Taylor began trembling uncontrollably, knowing that this man who could nearly blow up a ship and get away with it would have no qualms at all about putting an end to his miserable life. His only hope was that Newport might not be willing to shoot him. That would bring the rest of the camp running in a hurry and it would get out that Newport had dynamite packed away with his belongings.

"What on earth are you trembling for, Mr. Taylor? I'm not planning to shoot you." Newport's eyes narrowed. "I merely came to retrieve what belongs to me. I see you have found it."

Taylor did not say a word. No lie was going to get him out of this mess.

"Mr. Taylor, if you would please set the bag on the ground, we can get this over with in a hurry. It is very late and I am sure you are as tired as I am."

Taylor did as Newport asked and placed the bag on the ground. Then he placed his hands over his head without being asked.

"That's very good, Mr. Taylor."

Taylor found the courage to ask a question. "What's your game, Mister? What are all those explosives all about?"

Newport smiled and gestured toward the man with his gun. "So, you've found my little package, have you? Well, that is none of your concern. Now, Mr. Taylor, if you would please step back into the water up to your waist."

"What for?" Taylor said, stalling for time. He weighed his options. He could yell for help and be shot for sure, leaving Newport to dynamite the camp. Or he could attack the man, but the result would be no different.

"I merely want to neutralize the weapons at your side. A barrel full of water ought to do the trick. Step back, please."

Taylor decided to do as the man asked. There still might be a chance of getting out of this alive as long as he did what he was told. He stepped back into the icy water until it reached past his gunbelt. "Aren't you going to shoot me now?" he asked sarcastically.

"I assured you before that I have no intention of shooting you. It would make far too much noise, and we wouldn't want to disturb the Indians surrounding the camp, now, would we?" Newport picked up the bag that lay on the ground and reholstered his pistol. "Thank you so much for minding my pack, Mr. Taylor. I'm sure there will be no further trouble regarding its contents."

Newport turned his back, leaving Taylor to wonder just what the man was up to. Surely he wasn't going to walk away and leave him standing there all night. He must know that Taylor would run straight to Morgan with the story.

It took Newport less than a second to turn and whip the knife into Taylor's chest, and not much longer than that for his target to die. Taylor tried to cry out as he fell, but all that came out was a muffled gurgle from somewhere in his throat. As he hit the calm water, he was trying to pull the blade from his body, yet the twitching of his arms told Newport that he was already dead.

"Good night, Mr. Taylor," Newport said. "I think we will both sleep better now." Newport returned to his tent unnoticed, replaced the bag, and crawled back into his bedroll. He did sleep much more deeply, knowing that the crocodiles of Lake Gatun were having an early breakfast.

The next day, King was less concerned with map-making than he was with getting through the jungle with his hide. They stopped momentarily at various sites, and King took the scantest of notes. Their supply of quinine was running out and many of the men were nearly too ill to walk, much less carry supplies. Much was left behind.

There was so much fuss about getting under way, that Lee did not even notice that Taylor was missing until the noon meal, when he deliberately sought the man out. Lee looked throughout the camp, but there was not a trace. None of the other guards had seen him since the night before. Lee panicked. Newport must have caught him spying and quietly done something about it. Lee decided it was time to confer privately with King and O'Sullivan before they all ended up dead.

"What! Are you out of your mind, Morgan? You pulled me away from my work to tell me some fantastic story about one of your guards being missing. Just find him, dammit. We've probably got Indians crawling all over this camp and you want me to worry about one guard that wanders off into the night? What the hell was he doing out alone anyway, looking for bananas?"

Lee shook his head at the man's callousness. "This wasn't one of those two-bit thieves you picked up off the streets of New Orleans. I'm talking about Taylor, one of the best men we have, and the same one I assigned to keep an eye on Newport."

King forgot everything else on his mind. "Oh!" he said. "That's another matter altogether."

"What's this about keeping a guard on Newport?" O'Sullivan said. It was the first he had heard of this.

King spoke first. "Morgan thinks Newport had something to do with that fire we had back in New Orleans. Cook saw a man fitting his description carrying a black box, and Morgan seems to think Newport has the same kind of black box."

"That's right," Lee said, "except I know he has it. I saw it through Tim's camera. Even got a shot of it. I asked Taylor if he couldn't get a look inside when Newport was sleeping. Newport may have caught him in the act. If so, there's no telling what's happened to him."

"What do you suggest we do, Morgan? We can't just walk up and ask to look into the man's personal effects. Besides, we have no proof that he's done anything. There's nothing to go on but circumstantial evidence. We can't hold him for that, even in Panama!"

"I'm not suggesting we do anything," Lee said. "I want to see what he's up to and the best way to do that is not to let on that we suspect a thing. We make an announcement that Taylor's missing and leave it at that."

"I'm game," said King. "If we ever get out of here, we'll sort it all out then."

"Count me in," O'Sullivan said, "though I still don't have any idea of what's going on."

They hit the trail that afternoon. Their goal was to make half the distance to the camp by midafternoon. All day, Newport kept strangely to himself, and that fact did not go unnoticed by Lee Morgan.

They had not quite finished setting up camp in an open grassy area when the attack came. Maria was the first to see the signs. She spotted an Indian stalking the group, crawling through the grass, coming closer. Then she spotted another and soon the whole camp was pointing them out. Indians were moving in slowly from all directions. There was nothing to do but stand their ground and fight.

Lee Morgan had not been idle during this time. He quickly organized the men to build a shallow, circular wall, inside which the group could take cover and hold off the attackers as long as possible.

The first wave came from the side from which the explorers had come, and Lee cursed himself for not keeping a sharper watch behind them. The Indians had no fear. A group of ten rushed the encampment with rifles awkwardly blazing from their shoulders. The Indians were quickly cut in half by the Americans' superior firepower. The remaining Indians retreated into the brush to wait for the next onslaught.

"I thought these guys used blowguns," O'Sullivan shouted over the din of rifle fire.

"Only when they're not working for the railroad," Lee called back.

O'Sullivan knew he was probably about to meet his end, but through all the shooting, he found himself strangely wishing he could set up his camera to record the event.

"Hold your fire until you're close enough to hit your target," Lee called to the group. "That first wave was just to test the water. You can expect the whole lot of 'em to come charging in any second now." Lee looked around for King and Clarissa. King was lying next to O'Sullivan and looked like he was about to shake out of his socks. Clarissa was right next to him, her rifle at the ready and a determined look on her face.

Indians suddenly sprang up in every direction, all screaming and running toward the camp, some carrying guns and others not. Some were preparing blowguns and bows and arrows as they ran. Lee figured there must have been a hundred of them all together.

"Good Lord, would you look at them," O'Sullivan exclaimed. "Where the hell did they all come from? I didn't know there were this many Indians in the whole country."

"This ain't the half of it!" Lee shouted. "Look over there." He pointed to the large group on horseback approaching them from the north at full gallop.

King's eyes widened even more and O'Sullivan nearly fainted dead away.

Most of King's men were given shotguns. That way even those who had never handled a gun would be able to hit something. As the Indians approached, Lee let loose with his shotgun as soon as they were within range. The Indians were coming so thick that Lee's sawed-off could spray a couple of savages at a time with hot lead.

He did not waste a shot, reserving each until he

was certain he would not miss. Lee alone managed to put a big dent in their forces. As he glanced over his shoulder, he saw that King and O'Sullivan were holding their own. But the captain and Maria were not so luckly. The heaviest attack was from that side and men there were already engaged in hand-to-hand. Maria was having a hard time with the shotgun and Lee jumped up to help her. But just before he got to her side she was hit in the throat with a dart and dropped paralyzed into his arms. There was nothing he could do to save her. As she closed her eyes, she simply said, "Lee Morgan . . . thank you."

Lee set her gently on the ground and turned his anguish into fury. His Colts were blazing, sending a steady stream of lead into the melee. Indians and his own men were dropping everywhere. How could the railroad pay these men to fight with such passion? They freely gave their lives for the men that owned them.

Lee knew there was no way his people could win, but he was determined to go down like Custer if it came to that. He looked up at the advancing horses. They were almost upon them, and once they arrived, what was left of his men would be wiped out for sure. He wondered what would happen to his ranch, and if word would ever get back to the States about what had happened to the King expedition. There were only a dozen or so men left standing. The others were either dead or dying. Nearly half the Indians had gone down as well, and now they were regrouping for the final attack.

Johnson was dead, stabbed in the back while he

fought another savage. Nearly all of King's inexperienced party had been killed, and O'Sullivan had been wounded yet again, yet he bravely fought on. Lee saw that Newport was still alive and didn't have a scratch on him, and though he had been firing openly, Lee never saw him hit a thing.

While the Indians were gathering for their final strike, Lee looked at the men on horseback once again. They were heavily armed and riding directly between his men and the Indians. Then there was the spark of recognition.

The lead man on horseback was Narvez's general, the very man who had threatened them just a week before. The horses veered off and rode straight into the Indian camp. Bullets and bodies flew everywhere, the soldiers routing the Indians and sending them running off into the jungle once again. There was another party on horseback approaching from the same direction, and Lee suspected that this group would contain Narvez himself.

With the Indians dispersed, both groups converged on Lee's camp riding around in a loose circle to inspect the damage.

Lee wandered aimlessly around the camp, trying to see who had lived and who had died. O'Sullivan had fallen unconscious and Lee tried to find the doctor to tend to his wounds. He found him lying on his back with an arrow through his chest. King and Clarissa had made it through, and Newport was cowering behind a pile of boxes, looking very frightened, even more so than before the fighting had begun. Beside him was Cook, wracked with several bullet wounds but with a strange smile on his contorted face. The old coot sure got his last adventure, Lee thought.

What was left of the party, no more than fifteen men and Clarissa, gathered in the center of their crudely fashioned circle. Narvez rode up and dismounted, walking gravely over to King and Lee. "Gentlemen, I am sorry I could not get here sooner. I had not expected you to be attacked this soon. It was my belief that they would wait until nightfall. The Indians are far more stealthy then. I am very sorry."

"Well, at least you got here. There's a few of us left alive. We owe you thanks for that," Lee said. He was still stunned that Narvez had actually helped them.

"Gentlemen," Narvez said. "Please allow my doctor to tend to your wounded. We will remain camped here for the night and in the morning my men and I will escort you to the coast where you can meet the ship waiting for you."

"That sounds just fine to me, Narvez. I'll need your men to help get these bodies in the ground. We ought to have some shovels around here somewhere."

"Might I suggest a mass grave?" Narvez inquired. "I know it may sound distasteful, but we haven't much time and there is certainly much else to do."

King made an awful face at the thought, but consented. Lee went to Clarissa, who had been crying since the battle ended. Lee didn't know whether they were tears of sadness for those who had died, or tears of joy that she was still alive. His arm went around her shoulder. He sat on the ground with her and tried his best to get her to maintain control. There was still a long journey ahead of them and a hysterical woman wouldn't help matters.

Clarissa's eyes finally dried. "I could kill daddy for this," she said to Lee. "Why didn't he bring more men and guns if something like this was likely to happen?" She pounded on Lee's chest to make him understand.

"Don't be so hard on him. He had no way of knowing we were going to get a welcome like this. No one did. He brought as many men as the government allowed him. And he's done his best to keep this group together under stress. He did his share of shooting when we were attacked, too. He ain't no coward."

Lee couldn't believe what he was saying. Of course King had a choice. He could have halted the expedition at the first hint of trouble back in New Orleans. Or he could have changed his route or the date of the expedition. There had been a million things he could have done. But the man had so blindly trusted the government's word, so convinced there would be no problem, that he led his men—and his daughter—to almost certain death. Now Lee was practically telling this lovely girl that the man was a hero.

Clarissa nuzzled his chest, seeking solace in Lee's presence, a presence that had done more to protect them than anyone else who had come along on the trip. Clarissa was now openly admiring the man. He was feeling the closeness he had felt before she had scorned his advances. Lee Morgan was the man she had always wanted, but whom her father insisted she avoid.

"I'm so glad you're here, Lee. We'd probably all be dead right now if it hadn't been for you."

"If you want to thank someone for saving your skin, go shake Narvez's hand. He's the one that chased them Indians off."

Clarissa interrupted his sentence by placing a wet kiss on his open mouth. Lee responded in kind, kissing her passionately and hoping that King was too busy to be watching.

Lee broke away from the woman's increasingly persistent kisses. He held her from him and rose to his feet. "I've got to help bury those bodies. Are you sure you're all right? I can get one of Narvez's doctors to look after you."

"I'm quite all right, Lee," she said, brushing the grass off her plaid shirt. "And I didn't mean to get so . . . so emotional. After all, someone might see us and think you are kissing a boy!"

9

A foot of loamy soil lay on top of the mass grave. With Cook in it, the men who had just put away their shovels had to eat a supper of cold canned beans and dried fruit. No one felt much like cooking anyway. Several of Narvez's men had gone out on patrol while the grave was being dug, but when they returned they had nothing to report. Evidently, the Indians had realized their defeat and no amount of railroad money would bring them back. They had not known that Narvez's men would come to the rescue and were probably now reporting his treachery to the railroad executives.

Night seemed to come too quickly. A light guard was posted since Narvez did not seem to think that there would be another attack. The Indians had all but ruined the expedition and the railroad barons would probably not risk the lives of their own men on another attack of the heavily armed encampment. They had issued their warning and made their point clear. If Washington wanted to build a canal, they were going to have to fight to get it.

Lee lay awake in his tent thinking of how Narvez had taken over the entire operation. Better him than King, Lee thought. At least Narvez was a military man, and spoke his language. If King had remained in charge, he probably would have led them right into the Indian village. The expedition was over. There would be no more surveying, no more measurements taken. All that remained now was to get to the coast and be thankful that they had made it back with their lives. King would have a lot of explaining to do back in Washington.

And what was on Narvez's mind? Would he try to extort money from them once they reached the ship? Would he hold the other ship hostage or even kill them all to make amends with the betrayed rail owners?

Lee was thinking what a fool he was for letting Narvez's men have sole responsibility for guarding the camp when he heard a footstep outside his tent. His knife in one hand and Colt in the other, Lee rose to a crouch, ready to pounce on whoever entered. He suspected that it might be Newport, who had been acting suspiciously glum all evening. Perhaps the man was now going to try to get Lee out of the way.

The flap parted and Lee saw one of the most welcome sights he could have imagined. With her plaid shirt unbuttoned to the navel and wearing an even tighter pair of bluejeans than she had worn before, Clarissa stepped into the darkened tent.

Lee put his Colt aside and resheathed the blade, then he sat back on his bedroll and admired the woman. "Well, are you going to invite me in or aren't you?" Clarissa asked.

"If you leave, I'll come after you, like it or not," Lee said. "I was just laying here wondering what you wore under those duds. I doubt there's a petticoat tucked into them pants."

"Nothing," she answered and moved toward him. "But you'll never be sure until you look for yourself, will you?"

Lee took her by the wrist and lay her beside him. He held her chin in his hand and kissed her heatedly on the lips. "Oh, Lee, I've wanted you so. I tried to tell you that when we first met, but you didn't seem to take the hint."

Lee drew back from the woman wondering what she was talking about. "The only hint I took was when you barehanded me cross the jaw."

Clarissa looked ashamed. "You knew I was upset. I was worried about daddy then. It just wasn't the time. Couldn't you see that?"

Lee smiled at the woman as she explained. "Speaking of daddy," Lee said, "where is he now? I've never known him to let you out of his sight for more than a minute. You're not setting me up so he can come in here and blow my brains out, are you?"

"Of course not, silly. Lee, I want you. Didn't you see that on the ship before? Daddy's asleep. All the excitement today knocked him right out. A cannon wouldn't wake him up now. I practically screamed in his ear to see if he would wake up. Then I came straight here."

"Well, then," Lee said, "why don't I just see if you're lying about what you say is under those pants. I can see that you were telling the truth about the top part.''

"I assure you, Lee, I was telling the truth.''
Clarissa stretched her arms around him and they
both rolled in a heated embrace, Lee brushing her
lips with the intensity of his kisses.

He slid the shirt from her shoulders and over her
arms and Lee watched her white breasts sway as she
removed his. He cupped them in his hands and held
them high like an offering to the gods, then sucked
them gently until the soft, smooth nipples turned
taut and pointed. As Lee pulled away, Clarissa
arched her back and thrust them into his mouth
again, savoring the feel of his wet tongue against
her body.

"Oh, Lee, you simply don't know how much I've
wanted you. Every night I've lain in bed thinking
something like this might happen, but never dared
to make it happen.''

Lee knew how she felt. Though he didn't like to
admit it to himself, the sample she had given him
had served to make him want her all the more. Now,
with a broad hand behind her back, he was laying
her back onto the bedroll. His hand went
immediately to the buttons of her pants. They fit
her full hips so tight that she had to help him get
them unfastened. As she undid each button, Lee
folded the flaps back to uncover more and more of
her flat stomach until at last he reached the first
strands of blonde hair.

"Well, I see you're no liar,'' he said, then peeled
the pants halfway down her hips. Lee slid his hand
between the jeans and her milky skin, stroking the
wispy triangle of hair and inching his fingers toward
the wetness below. She gasped as he reached her

entrance and touched his finger on the swelling bulb guarding it.

"Do me easy, Lee. I want you to take me nice and slow." Lee had no intention of doing otherwise. They had all night and this Eastern woman who had so impassioned Lee shouldn't be given a thank you and a pat on the rear in return for satisfying him.

Clarissa arched upward against Lee's probing fingers and he took the opportunity to slide the pants around her knees. Lee's fingers slid easily into her. Clarissa began rotating her hips and groaning so loud that Lee thought one of the guards might come to investigate. Finally, she pulled his hand away from her.

"What's wrong," Lee asked. "Did I hurt you?"

"Of course not, silly. But I came here to give you pleasure too. I want to see what you have under those pants of yours as well."

Lee got to his knees and began unfastening buttons. At the sight of his black bush of hair, Clarissa's eyes widened. Then Lee let the trousers drop to his knees. His erection stood well out in front of him, relieved to be released from the prison that kept him away from her. "It's beautiful," Clarissa said, her eyes admiring the thick red shaft that throbbed as if it had a life of its own. "And tonight it's all mine."

Lee lay beside her once again, and she took the shaft in her fist and pumped the loose skin until it swelled even more.

"Oh, Lee, I want this inside me. I want to feel it shoot all in me. I can't wait any longer. I want it right now."

Lee started to straddle her, but she pushed him

back and turned away from him. He looked at her questioningly.

"Do it like this. Come in behind me. I've never had it like that before."

Lee didn't have to be asked twice. This woman definitely knew what she wanted. He moved in behind her and put his hand between her thighs, feeling the wetness that had seeped onto her legs. Lee pressed against her back and brought his hand around to massage her breasts, and Clarissa thrust her buttocks against his cock. She lifted her leg to let him in and Lee grasped his organ, rubbing the tip against her slit while stroking himself.

"Lee. Ohhhhh. Do it now. Put it all in me. I want it."

She was tight, but wet enough that he slid the entire length in with no trouble. Clarissa immediately began pumping her hips and Lee had to steady himself to keep from losing his balance.

Slowly, she rolled over onto her stomach and Lee followed her every movement, maintaining the rocking movement she had started. Once he lay directly on top of her, she rose to her knees. He followed, admiring the gorgeous body bending over in front of him. Lee was on his knees now, pumping her hips more quickly as her excitement increased. He felt the pressure building within him, and knew that this new angle would have him coming within seconds. He grabbed her cheeks and spread them to watch his cock sliding in and out of her.

Clarissa picked up the pace and Lee knew she was about to come as well. He reached beneath her and fingered her clit, rubbing it between two fingers. This was just too much.

"Ooohhh," she screamed. Clarissa clenched her thighs together and Lee slowed for a moment, knowing she had come. Her body was bathed in sweat, making it glisten in the dim light. When she recovered she lowered her head to the ground to rest. "Now it's your turn, and I want you to take me as hard as you want."

Lee pumped his hips even faster, watching every entrance and exit from her body. His balls were flying wildly until Clarissa reached back and held them, tickling the dark hair covering them. His body slapped against her loudly and he sank his fingers into her cheeks. He knew all at once he could not stop from shooting in her even if she had wanted him to and he slowed to make the feeling last all the longer. Clarissa gave his balls a squeeze and he spurted deep into her, feeling waves of fluid planting themselves in the depths of her cunt.

Spent and exhausted, Lee pulled out of her, and Clarissa gave a little gasp as his rod left her. He was coated with her juices and Clarissa quickly turned over to wipe him dry. She kissed him deeply once again and they both fell into each other's arms on the bedroll.

The night was quiet.

There was blood on Narvez's bedroom. The man's throat had been cut in the night. General Cienfuegos cursed himself for not keeping closer watch on his men. The revolutionary government was over and each soldier suspected the other of the treasonous act. Some thought it might have been Cienfuegos himself, making a bid for total control of the country.

King was shocked. How could this happen right in the midst of camp, with heavily armed men posted throughout the night? And worse, without Narvez's assistance, they might not be able to reach the coast. After the president had been buried, King reluctantly approached Cienfuegos with his concern.

"That is now your concern, Señor King. I have no control over these men now that el Presidente is no longer with us. They will now return to their homes and await the return of the Colombian troops. I am truly sorry, but that is the way it must be. Our leader has been slain, perhaps by one of my men—perhaps, even, by one of yours. There is no way to tell. I am willing to let you and your men leave for the coast, but do not expect further assistance from these men should you come under attack again. They will be on their way back to their families."

"You don't seem too concerned that your new government only lasted three weeks," King said.

"That is the way life is in Central America, Señor. Perhaps Presidente Narvez was not strong enough. There will be another man to lead us out of misery. Our people will not be stepped on forever."

"Well, please give your men our thanks for coming to our aid. I will see that we get under way immediately."

The two men shook hands and King returned to his men, instructing them to salvage what they could carry. The fifteen left in the party set out on foot ten minutes later. The coast was just a few miles away and there would be no more jungle to walk through. They could make it by midday if there were no delays.

They no longer had a guide to lead them, and King had to rely on his compass and maps to get them to the precise location where the ship was to pick them up. Everyone prayed that the ship had not come under attack as well.

Lee Morgan had no doubt that it was Newport who murdered Narvez, but kept his idea to himself. If they were to still get out alive, he would have to keep his own men from coming under suspicion. Newport would be dealt with once they reached the States, even if it meant that Lee had to go to Washington to testify.

At last the coast was sighted, but no one was elated. The ship was anchored in the bay, and King thanked the heavens that his reading of the map had been accurate. The entire party was still wary of another attack. If the railroads were as powerful as everyone thought, it would be a simple task to post more Indians in the tall grass surrounding the beach, and without the help of Narvez and his men, their small party wouldn't stand a chance.

The beach was reached without incident and Lee started a bonfire to signal that the men aboard should come and pick them up in the lifeboats. Lee had just gotten the fire started when he saw the body wash up. This was no Indian. The man had definitely been an American.

Lee thought the worst. What if the boat had come under attack and was controlled at this minute by Indians? Lee saw the lifeboats being lowered into the water, but the ship was too far out for him to tell who was in them. Then he saw the huge black spot on the upper deck, as if the ship had suffered a fire.

There was now no question—the ship had been attacked. But who was coming to greet them? There were several boats and each was manned by two men. If they were hostile, there were certainly not enough of them to take on even King's meager party.

"Everyone take cover in the grass, until we see what this is all about. If those aren't American faces in those boats, open fire as soon as they reach shore," Lee shouted.

But they were American faces, and smiling at that. Lee stood as they got out of the boats and walked around the fire, wondering what had happened to the group.

"Hello, there," Lee shouted.

"Are you King?" the leader of the men shouted back.

"Not even a prince," Lee said, a big grin on his face as he walked toward the men. Everyone else stood and walked toward the group on shore.

"What happened to your ship?" Lee asked.

"Indian attack! Last thing we was expecting out here in the bay. Damn near took us, too. Fools came out here in the middle of the night on rafts. Couple even managed to get on board and set a couple of fires before we ran 'em off. Where's the rest of you? We were told that there'd be near fifty."

"Dead and buried," Lee said. "We didn't get so lucky."

"Sorry to hear that. But get aboard. We'd better get moving before those savages decide to try something else."

Thirty minutes later they were all aboard and moving quickly through the bay toward Nicaragua and home. No one was more relieved than King. His assignment had been a complete failure and now he would have to go back to Washington in embarrassment. But at least he was alive and had the most important piece of information he could bring back in his head. It was not going to be an easy task to build a canal across this deadly country.

Clarissa, too, was relieved. Yet her research into the Indians for her thesis was a disappointment. The only thing she had learned was that all the Indians here were backward savages under control of the railroads—not much of a theme for a paper she had once hoped would be published.

O'Sullivan lay in the sick bay half conscious while the doctor tended to his many injuries and the consumption that had nearly killed him. He vowed that if he ever made it back, he was going to move east and open that little portrait studio, but Lee knew that O'Sullivan had too much gumption to carry out the threat.

They were moving out of the bay and into the Pacific near dusk. As many as were able were above deck watching the scarlet sunset streak the sky. In just over a day they would be in Nicaragua, not home, but a far safer place than where they were. Lee reminded himself that he would have to pay a surprise visit to Lisa when he reached New Orleans.

At dinner that evening, Lee stood up at the table right in the middle of a forkful of pork and beans. He strode straight out of the mess hall, leaving his plate where it lay, the other diners staring after him, wondering what was on his mind.

Newport was on his mind. All of King's party

were having dinner except Newport. Where was he? In fact, no one had seen him since he retired to his assigned quarters right after they arrived on board. Lee went immediately to his cabin and knocked. There was no answer. The door was unlocked and Lee stepped inside. The room was empty. Newport's gear was gone.

Lee rushed back to the main deck and saw the man just as he was stashing his bags beneath the canvas coverings of one of the lifeboats. Lee watched him as he made sure he was not being observed. Then Newport walked away as if he were enjoying the view from the deck.

Lee remained hidden. There was no need to approach the man. Lee knew exactly what he was up to. He was planning to leave the ship. Lee followed Newport at a distance as he returned to his cabin and latched the door. Lee knew the man would remain there until it was time to make his escape later in the night when everyone else was sleeping.

Lee now knew for certain what he had suspected all along. There was no need to ask questions. He just wondered how much time he had before the fireworks started.

He rushed down to the engine room, looking for what he knew must be there. It took him ten minutes, but he found what he was looking for— Newport's black box, neatly tucked under one of the huge boilers and covered with a cardboard box.

Lee didn't even have to look inside. He knew what he would find. Gingerly, he picked up the box and went above. He was just about to toss it over the guard rail when he reconsidered the idea. He threw the cardboard into the ocean and carried the black box to the lifeboat where Newport had placed his gear. Pulling out the canvas bag he had seen the man rummaging in earlier, he placed the box on top and pulled the drawstring tight. Then he replaced the bag and sat down out of sight to wait.

It was almost two hours later when Newport appeared. Almost without concern for getting caught in the act, he tore back the canvas covering of the boat, got inside, and began lowering himself with the pully. As soon as he hit the water, he untied the boat and began rowing quickly away.

Lee got up and went to the railing to watch. And he said nothing until the man was well away from them. Then Lee cupped his hands to his mouth and yelled, "Hello, out there!"

Newport looked up, startled. Lee Morgan had found him out. But then he realized that Morgan was too late, Newport was too far away for him to do anything to prevent his escape and once the ship had blown, Newport could row safely to shore and concoct another story for the folks back in Washington. "Have a pleasant trip, Mr. Morgan," Newport shouted back.

Newport smiled at his victory and laid the oars aside. The box he had placed in the engine room would explode at any moment and he was now going to enjoy the show. He picked up his canvas bag to get a piece of fresh fruit from inside.

Lee did not see the shock on the man's face when he opened the bag, but he did see the plume of water, wood, and flesh that shot thirty feet into the air.

"You too," Lee said quietly back over the noise of the explosion. Then he turned to go back inside.

Maybe he could find Clarissa King if she had not gone to bed.

Then his thoughts turned to Spade Bit and the woman who waited for him there. Maybe ranch life wasn't so bad after all.

Maybe Lee Morgan would go home to stay.